UNTRANSLATABLE

BY ALMA ALEXANDER

She looked up at the painting again, as though hypnotized by it. The loving eyes on the canvas were both a blessing on what she had sacrificed - renouncing what might have been less than perfect and holding out for that slice of heaven which the painting-bride promised could exist - and a never-ending reproach which stretched through her lonely years, for letting go of something which was not heaven but which might have given her an imperfect, possibly flawed, but human happiness. The painting had been a riddle, and Molly, throughout all the years she had been coming here, was yet to discover whether she had got it right. And now it was going to be taken, even that - years ago she had lost Willie at the command of the loving, lethal lady in white; now she was going to lose the lady herself. There had been no answers - and now, very soon, there would be no question.

Helpless, defeated, the old woman turned unsteadily and walked towards the door. The curator stared after her, his hands limp at his sides, his mouth open. Then he tore his eyes away and looked at the painting again - the hot blue eyes behind the veil, the reaching hand... He suddenly shivered.

"Take it," he said hoarsely. "Take it away and bury it some-where, deep. Let nobody ever find it again."

The young man bit his lip, turned, lifted the painting down, and laid it gently face down against the wall, blinding the blue eyes behind the veil.

There was a faint shape on the wall, a trace of where the painting had hung untouched for years; the wall looked curi-ously bare without it, almost indecent.

And the room was suddenly full of shadows, and then it was full of light.

- "The Painting", Alma Alexander

Trouvaille: Bucket List
An inventive (and nasty!) update on a classic story theme. It'll make you very nervous around empty buckets. —James Alan Gardner (author of ALL THOSE EXPLOSIONS WERE SOMEONE ELSE'S FAULT)

Mamihlapinatapei: Equinox
I've never been to a summer home, but this is so well drawn I feel like I have walked in this one. A wistfully beautiful story of golden summer and the unknown colder, greyer, other life, and the might-have-been magic promise of the equinox - that feels like one of my own memories. – Ryn Lilley, author of the Underground series

Inshallah: Night Train
"Night Train" offers us that rare sense of bittersweet hope for the future, one we may never understand but that believes in us. The universe is indeed perverse and all the more wondrous for it. –Sandra M. Odell, author of GODFALL & OTHER STORIES

Won: She Wore Yellow
"She Wore Yellow" is a look at all the half-glimpsed, half-remembered things that kick around the edges of our minds and torment us because we know they will all fit together if we can just remember the one missing piece, the elusive detail that we want to believe is real. A tantalizing story set on the knife-edge between memory and illusion. –Leigh Grossman, author of "The Green Lion" and "The Lost Daughters", creator of "Sense of Wonder"   "

CONTENTS

Komorebi: Color: 66
(Japanese)—the quality of dappled sunlight shining through trees—the interplay between the light and the leaves

Mångata: Go Through: 79
(Swedish)—the word for the glimmering, roadlike reflection that the moon creates on water

Aware: Leaving Via Callia: 87
(Japanese)—the bittersweetness of a brief and fading moment of transcendent beauty

Inshallah: Night Train: 99
(Arabic)—[in-shal-la] While it can be translated literally as "if Allah wills," the meaning of this phrase differs depending on the speaker's tone of voice. It can be a genuine sentiment, such as when talking to an old friend and parting with "We'll meet again, inshallah," or it can be used as a way to tacitly imply you actually aren't planning to do something. An example would be if someone proposes a meeting at 4 p.m., and you know you won't be able to make it on time. You can say, "I'll see you at 4, inshallah," meaning that you'll only make it on time if Allah wills it to happen.

THE GIFTS OF THE PAST

Won: She Wore Yellow: 112
(Korean) the reluctance on a person's part to let go of an illusion

Kintsugi: Something That Would Shine: 120
(Japanese): golden repair) is the Japanese art of fixing broken pottery with lacquer resin dusted or mixed with powdered gold, silver, or platinum (the "golden repair"). As a philosophy it speaks to breakage and repair becoming part of the history of an object, rather than something to disguise.

Ya'aburnee: The Flying Dutchman: 136

(**Arabic**)—Both morbid and beautiful at once, this incantatory word means "You bury me," a declaration of one's hope that they'll die before another person because of how difficult it would be to live without them.

Duende: The Painting: 144

(**Spanish**)—While originally used to describe a mythical, sprite-like entity that possesses humans and creates the feeling of awe of one's surroundings in nature, its meaning has transitioned into referring to "the mysterious power that a work of art has to deeply move a person."

Saudade: The Bones of Our Ancestors, The Blood of Our Flowers: 150

(**Portuguese**)—One of the most beautiful of all words, translatable or not, this word "refers to the feeling of longing for something or someone that you love and which is lost."

FOREWORD

Ethereal. Enchanted. Often magically powerful; frequently, hopelessly inadequate. Capable of building castles of clouds, turning lead into gold, making you hear a color or see the sound of the whispering wind in the silver shivers of aspen leaves. Capable of painting pictures without the touch of a brush or any paint at all, capable of building worlds without wood or water or stone, capable of making dreams solid enough to be touched and caressed, or of nightmares real enough to steal your breath away.

Language.

Words.

Meanings.

Language is such a heady incense for me, fragrant and glowing and vivid and bright. When I write, I tend to use words that people are sometimes forced to look up. I speak of the susurrus of wind tossed leaves; I know what petrichor means; I can use—properly and accurately—words like actinic, and etiolated, and flense.

I was very young when I first fell in love with the word, and your first love lasts forever.

And this love, for me, only deepened as I grew older, as I read more widely and more deeply, and as I began to write my own words, shape my own stories.

There were side roads that branched off the main thoroughfare of the language that I was using to do so, other languages, languages that spoke of other cultures, of delightfully strange and unfamiliar concepts and ideas, for which sometimes the primary language I thought and wrote in had no simple equivalent.

I had entered the Untranslatable Lands...and nothing would ever look quite the same again.

It becomes, at some point, impossible to see or experience something and not wonder how it might appear to someone who is not you, how a strange and different pair of eyes might interpret something that is utterly familiar to you or just how lost in translation a concept that seems simple to somebody else can become when you try to understand it from your own perspective.

There are words in other languages which require whole sentences, sometimes whole paragraphs, of explanation in English. And the attempts at translation transcend the language-to-language direct parallel lines. There are times when it is necessary to adjust one's entire understanding of the world to fully understand a concept which can at once be simple to one mind and unutterably complex to another.

That is one axis on which this collection rests—the attempt to take an Untranslatable Word and to attempt to give a glimpse into its bigger meaning through a story.

The story is not *about the word*. It is about that untranslatable concept behind the word. It's all about the quiet stab of comprehension—the *Oh! I see it now!* moment in which understanding breaks into a reader's mind like the light of dawn cracking the edges of shadowed and unfamiliar landscapes and illuminating something that is almost, almost, *almost* within their grasp.

It is a literal journey, into language landscapes of Japan, of Sweden, of the frozen wastes of the far north where the Eskimos roam, of France, of Portugal, of Tierra del Fuego. A glimpse into the worldview and the mindset of cultures different enough from our own to produce a single word that encompasses a world of concepts.

The other and somewhat unexpected axis turned out to be that of time—because these amazing, astonishing, delightful, enchanted words seemed to fall naturally into categories which indicated a quickening anticipation (a beginning), a startling awareness of the moment in which one finds oneself drawing breath (the middle) or a quiet looking back on things that were but no longer are, often sorrowful and regretful, sometimes melancholy, sometimes just coupled with a pang of a sense of something that's passed away (the end).

And so the stories in this collection found their place in space and time and language.

Translating the Untranslatable.

Alma Alexander

SOMETHING IS BEGUN

IKTSUARPOK

BLACK WINGS OVER KJELLMAR

NOTES ON THE WING-BORN OF KJELLMAR
MOBILE AMBASSADOR GELLMAN GRON ABALAS

There had been some curiosity, before I came here, as to the appearance of the Kjell. They are humanoid, but they are plumed from the top of their head all the way down their solid neck which broadens into wide muscled shoulders and onto their backs, spilling over the shoulder and running down a feathered line diagonally across their pectoral muscles until they peter out mid-abdomen. Male and female alike wear colorful kilts, leaving this upper part of the body bare. Some Kjell, of the higher social order, have a spectacular crest—it remains unclear whether it is the crest, randomly obtained by genetic lottery, that provides the entry into the upper social echelons, or if it is that the members of that particular class are a separate subspecies who are born with the identifying crest in place.

The feathers range in color from dowdy browns to brilliant burnt oranges and reds, and one family line which boasts plumage which is so deeply red that it begins to fold into purple and even traces of blue on some edges. (Illustrative images enclosed as attachments to this report.)

But these plumed and feathered creatures had no wings underneath the back feathers, not even vestigial ones hidden under cover of plumage. It was an obvious question, and we asked; there was a great reluctance to discuss the question, and we had allowed the matter to drop for the time being, until I could perhaps find a better opportunity to inquire about it.

I arrived on Kjellmar in the spring of what they identify as their year 11432 (reference: the period which they call a year is roughly 1.75 times as long as the standard year as measured by the original Terran base unit). Our initial encounters with the Kjell were borne out by my extended stay here—they are a closed and mistrustful people and they dislike, even resent, strangers who intrude into their world. For almost five months after my arrival I had almost literally gotten no further than receiving terse acknowledgments from the servants assigned to my compound; I had studied their language before I arrived and I could make myself competently understood when I spoke it but nobody would answer me in the same language, responding to any overtures of my own in whatever they could muster of my own language—or, if they could not come up with the vocabulary or enough of an intent, with silence.

It was a lonely time, and I had begun to seriously question my presence or my usefulness on this world before I quite accidentally stumbled into a deeper layer of their society, one which they'd clearly had no interest in sharing with an outsider such as myself.

A winged one was born in my compound, to one of my own servants, and whether or not it was a fortunate thing to have happened, I was present in the house when the child was born, I observed the circumstances surrounding its birth, and I had questions which I insisted that I find the answers to. The time for silence was at an end.

They had not expected me to emerge from my quarters that late at night, and it was perhaps that which had made them err— they had been too intent on getting the newborn out from under my potential observation as quickly as they could, and they had sacrificed, in their urge for haste, a more adequate concealment. Thus it was that I quite clearly saw the infant they carried, and I quite clearly observed the shape of tiny wings on its back.

They were intent on their task and they did not immediately notice my presence as they hastened towards the spiral stair which led to the flat roof of the compound. One of them, the one bringing up the rear, turned at the last moment and saw me— and followed the others into the doorway which led into the stairwell, speaking quietly and urgently to those already inside. I had already decided to follow them, and the warning, if such, had arrived too late—I emerged onto the rooftop in their wake, and I was in time to see something that none of our inquiries had brought to light. A winged Kjell awaited on the roof, under the stars. I was in time to see the newborn child hurriedly handed over to the winged visitor, who carefully placed it in a pouch securely strapped across its abdomen and launched skyward, spreading immense wings which blotted out the view of the bright stars for a moment before the creature rose high enough to diminish, and then vanish out of sight.

I was aware that I may have crossed a line and stepped into some taboo—but they had accepted my presence there as Ambassador from the Coalition, and in the time that I was on Kjellmar they had learned enough of me to know that I could not permit this to pass without an explanation.

It was one of the compound staff, a high-ranking crested Kjell leading the small knot of Kjell who had made their way to the roof with the child, who made a short sharp gesture to the others, and then lifted his big round eyes with their large golden irises to me.

"I will need to find out more," I said, in formal Kjell.

"Yes, Ambassador," the Kjell said, in his own language, communicating with me at last. "I will see to it in the morning."

I did not sleep very well, very nearly not at all. In the morning I repaired to my office, and waited there for the Kjell to make good on his word of the night before.

When he did arrive, it was to invite me to accompany him out of the compound—and I did so, on his assurance that I could expect answers at our destination. That turned out to be the last house, a dead-end alleyway off one of the streets leading from the main marketplace. It was an unremarkable enough destination, with the door in need of a good coat of paint, except for the unusual fact that the house to which this door provided entrance was higher than its neighbors, its roof out of sight from any casual watcher. That might have given me fodder for thought, but at a gentle knock the door was opened and my Kjell guide and I stepped inside. He gestured me towards a doorway which led to a stair much like the one in my own compound, except that this one was two stories high, and I was a little winded when I stepped out into the room at the top of it. I took a moment to collect myself and in that moment the Kjell who had brought me here emerged into the room behind me, and I realized that the two of us were not alone in that room.

Another Kjell stood a few paces away from the stairwell opening, a pair of brindled wings folded down along the broad back.

We looked at one another in silence for a long moment.

"Why did you bring her?" the winged Kjell said, in their own language.

"She saw," my household Kjell replied, in the same tongue. "Last night, on the roof."

"That is no reason. She could have been told not to speak of it."

"She saw," my Kjell repeated, with a definite tone or resignation. "This one, she will not let it rest. I judged it best to let her speak to you."

They clearly did not know just how much I had learned, how much I could understand. Well, but that might have proved useful—and so I chose to eschew their language in favor of my own, when I spoke.

"So, there are winged ones," I said.

"We do not like to speak of it," my household Kjell said, in my own language, turning to me. "Not to outsiders. This is Kadora. I have brought you here to her so that she can answer the questions you must have. But this is a private matter, and we are much grieved that it has been permitted to be observed. In the light of the events of last night, however, it was considered necessary to at least prevent speculation. "

"When we came to your world—" I began, but the Kjell lifted his hand.

"We agreed to provide your Coalition with an embassy, and with information," he said. "But, as I said, this is a private matter. In time you would have discovered the existence of the winged kind—but perhaps in a context which would not have given you the misgivings of last night. The child is safe, and unharmed. This is our way."

"We have no wish to intrude..." I began, but Kadora shook her head, mantling the wings a little.

"You have seen and now you have questions and we know your kind," she said.

"My kind?"

"You are not the first to have come here, from Outside, and all outsiders are alike," she said, somewhat disconcertingly. The words were flat, inflectionless, and yet they had a certain quality to them that was at once resigned and threatening. One might have interpreted the utterance to mean that others had come but none had stayed for long—or that their stay here had been shortened by the Kjell themselves if they judged that necessary. All at once this concession to my interest and curiosity began to feel rather more like an audition as to whether I would be permitted to stay or forced to leave, and just how much I would be permitted to divulge of what I had learned.

But I would learn what I could, until such time as I was barred from learning more. That was, after all, why I was here.

"The wings." I gestured to hers. "May I take a closer look?"

Kadora unfurled them, a little, a wordless invitation, and I stepped closer.

The pinions were large, well defined, with sharp primary feathers which looked almost as though they bore honed knife-edges. I regarded the wings with a certain respect, after this, because if true they could be deadly weapons. But Kadora did not threaten, just submitted patiently until I stepped back again, and then met my eyes.

"You have questions."

"Are all infants born winged...?"

Kadora shook her head. "Only a few," she said. "There aren't many of us, bearing the wings."

"I have never seen any—child or grown..."

"We do not live amongst our wingless kindred," Kadora said. "As you are already aware, because you have never seen us in the open in the settlements on the ground. There is always a House for us, like this one, where two or three of us dwell in seclusion—in readiness for a winged birth, like you saw last night, so that we can bear the winged child to where it now belongs. For us, there are eyries. Winged ones are taken from their dam as soon as they are born, and they are fostered and brought up there, among their own winged kind, and when they fully fledge, taught to fly."

"You do not have contact with your families here?"

"We do not have families here, not after we are taken from them when we are born with our wings. Our family is those who surround us in the eyries."

"You *never* come down among them?"

"We do," she said. "Once a year. On the last night of summer, on Flight Night, when we all come together, and the wingless ones take winged lovers that night. This is what you would have found out anyway, in the fullness of time, when the next Flight Night comes. This is what they always find out, the outsiders."

There was a complexity here which I could not immediately unravel. The Kjell Flight Night rituals were not exactly hidden— if I had known to ask about it I probably would have had my questions readily enough answered—but it was also clearly a subject on which they did not appear to wish any outsiders weigh in on, or take too close a look at. It was a ritual, a festival, and a biological compulsion—an occasion that brought reverence, acceptance, and shame all at once.

"Is that how the winged ones arise?" I asked quietly, aware I was probing what might be a forbidden spot—but I was Ambassador, and asking questions was what I had been sent here to do.

"Sometimes that means that wings come, when the child is born," Kadora said, a touch unwillingly. "We, winged women, we cannot bear. We are sterile. But the males can sire winged children on the Fledgeless and so our numbers are maintained."

"But there is congress between... between the wingless men and the winged females? You said, the wingless ones take winged lovers—both men and women?"

"Yes, we winged females take Fledgeless lovers," she said, mantling her wings a little. "They seem to find it exciting. And for us there is no danger because they cannot impregnate us."

"Do you actually… fly… then?"

That was a stupid question to ask and I knew as soon as I uttered it—she had spoken of eyries, after all, and of winged babes being taken there, and I had seen one of them—perhaps Kadora herself, I had no way of knowing—take flight from the Embassy compound rooftop only hours before. But she seemed to understand what I really wanted to know, and answered that question instead.

"We can fly great distances," she said. "Sometimes the Fledgeless seek us out, and entrust us with messages, or even cargo—we are strong, we can carry a net bearing considerable weight if necessary. And we can reach the Seven Archipelagos much faster than a ship can." I nodded, for this began to explain a lot of things we had not yet found answers to in this culture—to wit, how news reached the scattered Archipelagos faster than we knew ships could get there. We had speculated about messenger birds—but we had simply failed to take that to its natural conclusion. "In exchange they leave us alone, otherwise," Kadora continued. "And we use the wings… for our own purposes."

A certain smile had drifted onto her features at those last words, a languor, and I thought I understood. It was crass to ask but I was here to learn.

"You use the wings in… pleasure…?Amongst yourselves?"

"We play in the sky," she said. "Out there above open water, or deserted islands where no eyes can see. Oh, it is glorious to love in the sky."

But they could not conceive their own children, their own winged children. So, they sired them on the… what did she call them?... the Fledgeless…

It was unexpectedly complicated. I asked questions which might have sounded stupid and ignorant, but I knew nothing, and I wanted to find out as much as I could before Kadora became disinclined to speak further.

"What are your own lives like? Do you form groups? Families? How are the new winged creatures raised?"

"Every eyrie is its own family," Kadora said, patiently enough. "We get sorted… by appearance… all wings are indeterminate, until the adult primaries come in, when the child is ten, eleven years old. And then the color of the primaries determines if that child stays with the eyrie which had raised it, or moves to one which matches its coloring."

I indicated her own wings. "Yours?"

She mantled them again; I found it almost hypnotic to watch them quiver ever so slightly as she stood there as though she was keeping them from flashing open and taking her away by main force of will.

"I am of the Brown Eyrie," she said. "I am Second Moult, of the Brown Eyrie. To the south of us, in the Archipelagos, there are Red Eyrie and Amber Eyrie, and others. And then there's the one furthest north. The White Eyrie."

"The White Eyrie?" I repeated. In my mind iconic images had begun to emerge, of humanoid creatures with white wings, angelic avatars which appeared to be part of the lore and mythology of almost every culture we had ever encountered. I found myself wondering how deeply rooted the imagery went—and Kadora confirmed some of what I was thinking, in her very next words.

"They are a strange lot—they don't mix with the rest of us often, only on Flight Night do we see them in any number, but they are the ones trusted with the deepest secrets, the highest honors. They do not carry cargo, nor do they carry love letters between lovers on different Archipelagos or messages to ships out to sea. They fly for Princes and for Priests. They are their own." She paused. "And then there's..."

She clamped her mouth shut on what she had been about to say, sharply, as though biting off the words she would have spoken. But I had noticed, and now of course I had to know.

"There is another?" I probed.

Kadora threw me a smoldering look. "We do not speak of it," she said.

I said nothing, but waited, and she finally sighed.

"For some," she said, "the wings grow in... black."

"What happens to them?"

"They fly away," Kadora said darkly.

"The Black Eyrie...?"

"They do not have an eyrie. They are solitary. They go where they go, and they do what they do, and none know where, or what. And the worst of it is…"

Again, the pause. But they had sent her here to give me straight up the information they knew I was going to spend my time digging for, and it was better, in their eyes, maybe, to give me their truth rather than let me learn some twisted version of it by finding it out in puzzle pieces from people who didn't know what needed to be told.

"The worst of it is what?" I inquired gently, assured that sooner or later I would be told, because I would ask until I was.

"The black… can come in any time. At any Moult." Kadora's lips were tight, as though she was trying to spit the words out through as small a space as she could, permitting only the bare minimum required to escape. "Any one of us, at any eyrie, can wake up one morning in the Moult and see the black feathers coming in where we had been brindle, or gold, or even white. And if that happens… it's exile."

"Twice exiled," I said. "First torn from mother's arms as babes, and then thrown out of the eyrie families if the black feathers come. That's harsh. Why do you drive them away?"

"I don't know," Kadora said. But there was fear in her eyes now. "They are different. They are dangerous. They are predators. They kill."

"Have you ever known one?"

"No. None of my Moult has grown black feathers. Nor of the generation above me. And the ones below are still in their first moult, the baby plumage. In my eyrie, not for a long time. Maybe we are blessed."

"Then how do you know what they are, what they do?"

"There are stories," Kadora said darkly.

"Who tells them?"

"The White Eyrie keeps the records."

I would never be permitted access to those. They would not be for the likes of me. But I felt pity for the black-winged creatures who were driven out of their society to forage alone and fend for themselves, solitary and isolated in an entire world that revolved around families and kindreds. It seemed to me that the only way left for them was to kill, because their lives were otherwise empty of love or companionship.

"Do they come to Flight Night?" I asked

Kadora reared back. "They would not be permitted," she said. "We would protect the Fledgeless from them. We would have to. That is our compact."

Alone, and not permitted even the glorious abandon of Flight Night. To bear black wings was to be outcast, and vilified, and feared. Damned.

I knew I would have to find them. To go looking for one of them. To hear their side of the story. I was sent as Ambassador to all of this world, after all.

Kadora could not or would not tell me how to go about seeking them. My household Kjell, who had withdrawn to give Kadora and myself the chance to speak in private, came for me not long after that, and I was escorted away from the house of the winged Kjell. I never saw Kadora again.

MOBILE AMBASSADOR GELLMAN GRON ABALAS,
Despatches.

She came out amongst them on Flight Night, the Ambassador from another world. The Kjell who milled about beside the bonfires, excited and more voluble than the Ambassador had ever seen them, even offered her an occasional nod of recognition, of greeting—they did not smile, the Kjell, but if they did there might have been a smile for the Ambassador that night. She had been amongst them for long enough for them to have learned her—she was curious, and persistent, and devoted to her duties, but she was also happy to learn and to abide by the rules.

Or so they thought, until that night.

When the winged ones came in their migrations from the eyries, the Brown and the Gold and the Amber and the Red and even a handful of dignified, solemn creatures from the White Eyrie to whom there was extended deference rather than welcome, the Fledgeless Kjell flocked to them where they landed, and the two kindreds laughed and embraced and mingled and celebrated the night when the divided Kjell were once again one, children taken from the arms of the women gathered here come down from the skies to which they were given to walk amongst their family of blood, the one kind to sate their longing for the other, with all permitted, all allowed, for that one night of the year.

But she hung back, the Ambassador, and she watched the skies. Long after everyone who might have been expected to come down from them had arrived, the Ambassador stood by herself, a little apart, watching the skies intently, as though waiting for something. For a while they remembered noticing her, seeing her there, but then the bonfire burned brighter and Flight Night grew louder and merrier, and the Kjell lost sight of the Ambassador, and interest in her doings that night.

By the time the bonfires had burned down and Flight Night was over and dawn was creeping over the horizon and painting the sea rose and gold, by the time they started waking, many hours later, the Kjell who had slept where they fell the night before, the Ambassador was gone.

They looked for her, because they were responsible for her, and they would have to account for her to the people who had sent her—but she had disappeared completely. They shrugged helplessly, the Kjell, when they gathered up her papers and belongings and handed them over to her people, after every search they could make had been completed.

But they did not tell the outsiders—they barely spoke of it among themselves—of the thing that they had found by the edge of the sea, on a lonely part of the beach where none had gone to seek their delights on Flight Night.

There had been footsteps in the sand, just above the waterline, the tracks those of the Ambassador's sensible wide-soled shoes.

And where the footsteps ended, three long sharp black feathers.

THE WORD BEHIND THE STORY

Iktsuarpok: (Inuit) the frustration of waiting for someone to turn up, the anticipation of constantly going outside to see if someone is coming

THE STORY BEHIND THE WORD

The anticipation of waiting for someone to come—well, what about the discovery about the black-winged ones, and waiting in frustration until you could find out, for yourself, just how much of what you'd found out about them was actually true...? Would you be outside—alone in the midst of a carnival, in the middle of a crowd which doesn't really know or care if you exist—waiting for that single someone whom you are expecting, whom you want to see, someone whose coming you are almost afraid of but which you find yourself anticipating with a strange, almost frightening thrill...? Again, you may find that you'd have to whittle the sharp edges off of this story peg to make it QUITE fit into this particular inspirational hole, as it were—but sometimes the fit doesn't have to be quite seamless for the idea to be put across. Sometimes, the light of illumination needs those tiny gaps to shine through.

IKIGAI

DREAMSHARE

Will you Dreamshare with me?

W Nang Sar could not believe that she had never heard those words before the strangers' boat came to her village. After... after, it was sometimes all she could do to remember a time when she had still believed that before the Moon was next full she would be a bride, that she would go from her wedding to a quiet little house where she would make a home for herself and for Sarav Iorn. A home to which he would come back every night after a day out on the ocean, led there by the light Sar had left in the window like all fishermen's wives did. A home where their children would be born in the fullness of time, and from which one day she could perhaps see her own daughter off to a wedding, crowned with water lilies and the scarlet blossoms of the *dhauri* trees.

But the strange boat had come. No fishing vessel, that; it had the clean, sleek lines of a racing craft—it might have seen better days, to be sure, dingy and neglected, its paint peeling and its brass dull, but it was a gentleman's boat which had never smelled of freshly gutted fish; its decks had never run with watery fish blood or seen the spill of scale and fin.

The villagers had come out to gape at it as it drifted into the shore, apparently guided by no conscious hand, only barely managing to come aside the tiny wharf without dashing itself to pieces against it. It was the local fishermen who threw a makeshift mooring rope over its pointed prow and left it bobbing loosely beside the wharf like a lost toy.

The first sign that there was indeed life on the boat came

many hours later, when a figure climbed slowly up on the unsteady decks from some fastness below—a wraith of a figure, ghostlike with an unseemly pallor and shrouded in long and loose red hair that fell in tangled waves about her face and shoulders. She was wrapped in the remains of something that had once been long and flowing and regal but which now lifted and stirred in the evening breeze in shredded streamers, revealing glimpses of pale leg and long narrow white arm.

The pale woman climbed to the deck and stood there weaving a little. And then the boat lurched with a sudden swell and she staggered, lost her balance without once losing the kind of eerie grace with which she moved, and fell silently backwards into the sea.

Two of the fishermen dove in and hauled her out. The sea water plastering the remnants of her garments to her body showed just how painfully thin she really was—the bones of her hips showed clearly through the clinging material, and her belly was a hollow underneath her ribs. She was gasping for breath when they brought her to shore, her long red hair darkened by water and falling wet and heavy against her lips and her eyes, but even then she only had those words in her mouth, those words and none other: *Will you Dreamshare with me?*

Sar had been there on the beach when they had brought the strange woman up out of the sea. She had heard those words. She had not known what they would mean to her. Not then. Not yet.

The fisherfolk had thought the lady was ill, and she had been taken to the healer's hut for help—but the healer was at a loss as to what to do with her. When he had swept the wet hair back from her face and looked into the wide eyes whose iris seemed to be all but consumed by the huge dark hole of the pupil and whose color—pale blue or gray—was barely hinted at around the edges of the black pupil, the healer had hazarded a guess that there must have been some drug involved, and suggested that she be taken to a pallet and constantly watched.

"But she could not have been alone," the healer said. "There had to be others on a craft that size. And if they are all like her, they all need help."

"We cannot walk uninvited onto another's boat," one of the fishermen had protested, the ancient laws of their lives an instinctive response.

The strange woman, who had been laid down on a pallet just within earshot of all this, moaned softly and turned her head as though she was in pain. The fisherman who had spoken flushed, cast his eyes down to his feet; the things which had been left unsaid—*if there are others, if they are all dead, then the boat is a prize*—suddenly seemed crass and greedy. But the woman on the pallet had not turned to react to what had been said. It was doubtful if she had even heard any of it. There was still only one thing on her mind.

"Dreamshare," she whispered, her voice husky.

"What is this Dreamshare?" one of the men who had rescued her asked, frowning. "That was all she could say, right from the start. Right until this moment. I don't understand."

"Neither do I," the healer said. "We will know more when she wakes."

But she never did wake again, the strange woman they had tried to save from the sea. She slipped into a fitful sleep, and then into something else again that made the healer sigh and shake his head. She died a little piece at a time, drifting off into silence, never waking to consciousness for even long enough to utter the invocation to the Dreamshare one last time.

She had not needed to. Before she was utterly gone from them, the village knew all too well what Dreamshare was.

The boat had not been abandoned after all. A few hours after the woman had fallen overboard another figure had managed to gain the upper deck, and this time it was a young man, naked except for a loincloth. His skin had been sun-browned once but it had started to lose the color and it was clear that he had not been out in the light for some time. He had not been as painfully thin as the woman had been, but it was obvious that he had already slipped some from what had once been a fine physique. And he had been more or less lucid.

He too had babbled about Dreamsharing for a while without making sense before he was finally brought back to a more coherent state, and the closer he came to that, the greater the hunger for the Dreamshare drug that grew in his face and in his feverish gaze.

"There is still some left on board," he told the healer, eventually. "There has to be. I need to go back. I need to find it. I need to..."

"How did you come to this village?" the healer had asked.

"The sea brought us, after we entered the Dreamshare—we did not guide ourselves after that," the man from the boat said. "To be honest I don't even remember our setting sail at all—one of us had to have cast off, cast us adrift, but I have no recollection of it. One does not travel *this* world when sailing the Dreamshare seas..."

He led the fisherfolk back to the boat, in the end. He invited them aboard. They found a third companion below decks, dead for some time and starting to smell; his remains were decently disposed of together with the ill-fated woman's. The village folks were left to deal with the dead; the survivor from the strange boat was far more concerned with ransacking the interior of the boat for something that had a far greater value to him than the lives of his companions.

He found it. Just enough of it to matter. Enough Dreamshare powder, a dusting of a pale jade green at the bottom of a cutglass vial, to make his cheeks flush a hectic scarlet and his eyes grow hot and hungry.

And he had said them, too, those strange words that had been on the lips of the woman who had died. But he had been lucid enough to make clear their meaning.

"Will you Dreamshare with me?" the stranger had asked a young fisherman who had happened to be beside him when the vial with the green powder had been found. And then, when met with a blank stare, explained. "This is not a drug to be taken alone. This opens the doors only to shared worlds, it will show you wonders you have never believed possible to imagine—because they never had been possible to imagine before, not by you, not by you alone. But when two come together—or even three, or more—it is sublime, it is unspeakably wonderful, and there are more strange and wondrous things out there than can ever be explored in a single lifetime but you have to try, you have to go back again and again, because each time there's just that *glimpse* of something out of the corner of your eye and it's greater and more beautiful and more glorious than that which you had been exploring on your previous trip—so you go back, chasing that, and maybe you find it but yet it shows you a third thing that you have to go back for and learn and see and own, or else you go back to a different place entirely, somewhere you had never been before and would have never believed you could go, never believed it existed if someone had tried to tell you of it before you saw it with your own eyes... Will you Dreamshare with me?"

"All right," Iorn had said, his curiosity fatally piqued. Iorn, Sar's Iorn, her chosen one, the man Sar had been pledged to since they were both children, with whom she would have spent the rest of her days in happiness and contentment had the drifting boat not come into their bay. The boat with the poison called Dreamshare.

The only reason Sar knew about any of this was because there had been another man present at this exchange. Iorn's friend Manam Dor had been present on the boat when it had happened, had seen it all, heard it all. But he had not been invited to join the pair who shared the last remaining grains of the Dreamshare powder. There had not been enough for three.

He had been jealous and angry, and had left them there, and in the throes of his resentment he had said nothing of it to anyone—but Iorn had not come back to his father's house that night. That night, or ever again. The evening after that, when the fishermen had come home from their day on the waters, the strange craft had gone, taking its surviving crewman and two of the folk from the village—Iorn, and Fanu Maira.

Maira's youngest brother, a lad of barely five, had been the only witness to what had happened to Maira—it was not clear from the boy's account of the events whether Iorn had come looking for Maira specifically or if she had just happened to be in the wrong place and the wrong time when he had come looking for a woman, *any* woman, to take into the Dreamshare with him. Maira had never been considered beautiful—her skin was darker than was considered fashionable and she could not seem to grow her hair long enough to braid into the maiden-crown cornrows that Sar and the other virgins of the village wore; it had been beyond the boy-witness's ability to discern, but there was probably a little bit of that in Maira's consent to go with Iorn. It was only after the boy's confused and garbled account of what he thought he had seen, that Dor had stepped forward and told of what he knew.

Sar thought that she would have gone, too, if it had been Iorn who had asked. But he had not asked. As far as she could tell he hadn't even made an effort to try and find her. He took the first willing female who crossed his path.

Will you Dreamshare with me?

Apparently, the dream she had been waiting to share with him had not been enough. Not after he had had his first taste of the drug.

Sar never quite knew how or why she had conceived the idea of going after Iorn. She didn't have much to go on—the name of the drug, Dreamshare, and the name of a single place which the stranger from the boat had let slip in an unguarded moment: a city called Cirian, the source of Dreamshare. Iorn had already had the Dreamshare in his system when he and his companions had set sail; they might have been making for Cirian, or their destination could have been somewhere quite different, but with the Dreamshare as their navigator it was not clear that they could have been making for any particular port at all. But it was a beginning.

Sar's father, Nang Samar, had forbidden her to leave the island when he found out about her plans.

"He is *gone*, Sar-*bib*," Samar had said. "It's over. You saw what that thing did to the others."

"They were others," Sar said stubbornly. "They were not Iorn. Iorn can fight this… he can fight it, if I find him, if I can bring him back."

"You don't know that," Samar said grimly. "Even if you found him at all, which is about as likely as your going out by yourself and landing a *baba-gar* fish with your own two hands."

Baba-gar could grow to be huge, dwarfing both boat and human, and when they were hunted it was usually with an organized flotilla of craft and a hundred fishermen—and then the mammoth catch, if they succeeded, was towed back to the shore by at least four or five boats. This was a village-sized operation, and the concept of dainty, diminutive Sar wrestling with a *baba-gar* was an image of epic failure. But instead of being discouraged by the idea, she had merely smiled at her father.

"Even *baba-gar*," she said gently, "are born and are babies in the beginning. If I wait, if I let Iorn disappear completely, it is indeed going to be a grown *baba-gar* of a problem—but if I leave now, maybe the trail can still be followed. It's still a baby *baba-gar*. I can grapple with that."

"And I say you will not go and waste your life on chasing a mirage," Samar had declared. "You are still my daughter, and I forbid it."

"Your daughter, who would have been a wife," Sar reminded him. "If they had come just a little later, the strangers, I would have been a widow. Able to decide for myself. Think of me as a widow, *papi*."

And she had gone away to be by herself, and cry, because she wasn't nearly as certain as she had made her father think she was. She was afraid… but there was a tiny light deep inside of her that she could not extinguish. A light of pure faith. If she went, she could make it right. The village was already thinking of her as a widow; she and Iorn had been too close to being wed. Sar could see the other young men in the village look away from her in awkward embarrassment if she caught their gaze on her. This was what it would be like. She was the ghost, caught on the cusp of being the bride and being the new widow, twice forbidden, and she knew she would still be the new widow when she was old and toothless and half-blind, even if she had never known the touch of a husband.

They had taken more than Iorn from her, the strangers. They had taken an entire life, meticulously woven and planned and prepared for, leaving Sar with nothing but the bitter aftertaste of memories never made. Her father might have believed otherwise but Sar knew that she had very little to lose by going after this particular *baba-gar*. There was nothing else that she could do.

She defied her father, turned her back on her village; a sympathetic fisherman from the next village down the coast ferried her over to the peninsula where the Big Town was, the place the villagers used to go every Great Moon to sell fish and shells and necklaces that the women had made out of coral and crystal and stone. Sar had never been there alone, and when the familiar little cockle boat pushed off from the stone wharf of Big Town to return to her island home she fought a sense of pure panic and a violent urge to scream for him to come back, that she could face it after all, that she could face whatever came for her in the village far more easily than she could face the big unknown that now stared her down with what seemed to be a malevolent loathing.

But she was here for Iorn, and it was Iorn's eyes that she saw staring at her next, the way they crinkled at the corners when he smiled at her, the way they seemed to contain the warmth of the sun in its heaven when they rested on her.

"And so he needs me now," Sar whispered to herself, bracing herself against fear, against loss of faith.

She asked about Cirian in Big Town. Nobody seemed to know about it, or would not say. People thought they had heard of places with names that were similar but when pressed these always turned out to be wrong, or unlikely. It was finally a glimpse of a gaunt man with dilated eyes and a hungry expression, so very like the woman from the strange boat who had died back at the village, that yielded Sar her first shred of hope.

"Cirian?" the man had repeated to her when she had accosted him to ask, and his voice was at first just as puzzled as all the rest. But it turned out that he had been puzzled for different reasons, because he continued, "What are you looking for in Ancirian-Shaba, my young innocent?"

That was a new name, a different name. Sar filed it away in her memory.

"I am looking for my betrothed. Sarav Iorn. He was taken from our village by someone… by someone who asked him to Dreamshare. They said the city of Cirian…"

But the man was laughing softly, softly and bitterly, and would not meet her eyes.

"You would not last a brace of hours in Ancirian-Shaba," he informed her. "You don't understand Dreamshare, if you are seeking to pull someone already in its grip out from the addiction. I have been without for less than a day, and look at me, look at my hands…" He held them out, and they were visibly shaking. "If I thought that you had any on you, I would have killed you for it by now if you had not volunteered to share it. But it's obvious you know nothing about the code."

"I can learn about the code," Sar said. "Tell me what I need to know."

Her companion stared at her for a long moment, his gaze full of bitter understanding and pity. And then he looked away, and sighed, and would not meet her eyes again.

"You know Dreamshare is a thing that seeks companions? You seek others, others seek you. The code… lets them, and you, know what you have found when you meet one another. Earring in left ear means you are looking for a man. Earring in the right ear, a woman. Both ears, you are not particular about your companion's gender."

"No earrings…?" Sar said, her fingers reaching out to touch her bare ear.

The man gave a short bark of a laugh. "You don't belong here," he said. It was not an indictment; it was an answer to her question. Wearing no adornment in her ears meant that she was not seeking anyone at all, and for the world of Dreamshare that meant that she was out on the sidelines, looking in.

But he went on, relentlessly—she had asked, and he would give her the whole of the answer.

"Rings on your fingers," he said. "Existing connections. Right hand, present. Left hand, past, your Dreamshare history. Index finger, male companions. Fourth finger, female companions. No more than three; three rings on either finger means that you have had—or are currently involved with—more than three companions. Black in a ring means that you are experienced, but do not wish to deal with newcomers; a ring with a stone on a middle finger of your right hand means that you are willing to take on neophytes, that you can teach. A ring with a green stone means that you have a supply of Dreamshare, or can get it. Those companions are prized. A ring with…"

"Stop," Sar begged, her eyes bright with tears. "All I want is *one* man, my man, my…"

"Ancirian-Shaba holds many men, and you may have to go through a considerable number of them before you even hear word of somebody specific. Are you sure you are up for this…? Have you ever *taken* Dreamshare before…?"

Sar shook her head mutely. Her companion shrugged his shoulders, turned away. His arms were crossed tightly over his chest, his hands tucked into his armpits.

"You will be dead by the end of your first night in Shaba," he said.

Sar bought an earring and a couple of cheap rings at a local bazaar the next morning. But the thought of finding the place she now knew as Ancirian-Shaba paralysed her with fear, with the shame that she might have to bring upon herself before she was through with her mission. Would Iorn even want her after what might happen there, if she found him? Would Dreamshare make him forgive her if she came to him stained by other men? Would Dreamshare let him even remember who she was… who she had been?

Would she herself forget, if once she was made to take the drug herself?

Was it even possible to contemplate finding Iorn without the possibility of losing herself?

But her feet were on this path now. She had no choice but to go on.

The Great Moon was waning before Sar finally found her way to the city called Ancirian-Shaba—it had taken her nearly fifteen frustrating days of hesitation and false starts.

When she finally reached the city, ferried (with every show of reluctance) into its harbor by a young man from a fisherfolk village not unlike her own home, her heart was beating painfully fast and her breath was loud in her ears. She had no real idea what to expect—by this time Ancirian-Shaba had taken on mystic dimensions for her, and she would not have been surprised to see her lost Family Gods walking its streets. She had never been to a really big city before and all her images were drawn from Big Town, the market, which by comparison with Ancirian was no more than a large village itself. Sar had merely extrapolated what she had known, made everything bigger, more intimidating, more overwhelming—but she did not realize how inadequate her imagination had been until she stepped off the boat onto the cobbled docks of the Dreamshare city and stared, intimidated, at the huge stone buildings that began just a little way ashore and seemed to go on forever, twisted into winding alleys that dove out of sight behind great buttressed walls, shimmering behind a veil of heat and a stench made of fermented grain, rotting fish, human sweat, and human fear.

There was a sense of slow ruin about it, as though she was looking at an illusion, as though the buildings only seemed to be standing but there was nothing there except blind windows and roofless halls and hungry shadows everywhere.

Three people converged on her from three different directions before she had taken more than a couple of steps from the water. Pupils wide, hands shaking.

"Will you Dreamshare…"

She lifted her hand, coded with what she hoped was still the correct message in the language of Dreamshare. "No—I'm looking for…"

They melted away, without another word.

Sar found herself letting out breath she had not been aware she had been holding. She realized that she had been half-anticipating an attack, even though they probably knew that she did not hold any Dreamshare powder, not newly arrived at the dock as she had obviously been.

It had been pure luck that she had avoided the drug thus far—but the luck did not hold, could not hold in a city like Ancirian-Shaba. Less than two hours after her arrival, hungry and thirsty and hopelessly lost, Sar stumbled over something that had looked like a pile of refuse at the mouth of an alley… a pile of refuse that unfolded into a rangy dark-skinned man with Dreamshare-hungry eyes and arms of whipcord. The arms folded around her, inexorable, pinning her down like a starfish; she struggled, but in vain. When one of the man's hands came swimming into Sar's panicked vision, it held a vial. A vial of a pale green liquid.

"Drink," the man said, his voice hoarse.

"No—no, I can't—I am looking for..." Sar resumed her struggles, but she might as well have been tied down with ropes.

"Drink," he said. "It's been nearly a day since my last Dreamshare. You are here, you are showing that you are looking for a man, drink."

"I *am*—I am looking for a man—but not..."

He wasted no further words. The vial was against her mouth, his other hand now twisted into her hair on the back of her head, tilting her head back. She gasped, tried to let the liquid that dribble over her lips and flow away harmlessly down her chin, but it was impossible. The Dreamshare juice flooded into her mouth, down the back of her throat; a fleeting and unexpected sweetness exploded in her mouth, and then it was gone, and a bitter aftertaste remained on her tongue and her throat burned with the passage of the drug.

And then it took her, a wave of warmth that spread from her throat over her shoulders and her arms, down her spine and into her hips and her loins. Her knees gave way; her hands spasmed helplessly against the dirty shirt of the man who held her, her lips parted with a soft sigh. She was aware that he had stepped back into the shadows of the alley without releasing his hold on her, that a single motion had swung them both against the brick wall at her back and then sliding down against it until they were lying on the pavement below, she underneath, he heavy on top of her lying between her thighs, fumbling at her breast and then pushing up her skirts as he guided himself into her.

Sar thought she might have screamed, but all that came out was a soundless whimper as he ground his hips against hers and the Dreamshare bridge solidified between them, taking them both into a strange country that she could not look at without gasping, a land which had a sky the color of a sandy-bottomed sea where fish darted through the clouds like birds, and plants waved gently in a breeze which might have been an ocean current. Jewels hung from the branches of strange trees which had no solid trunks—and small starfish scuttled through the grass at her feet. She could hear, far away, something that sounded like the crash of surf on the shore, and a strange fluting call which might have belonged to a bird. There were amazing, astonishing, unbelievable things everywhere she looked—and it all surrounded her, pervaded her, the sights and the sounds and the texture of smooth shell and sharp coral under her fingertips and the taste of fresh fruit just plucked from the tree and the salty smell of an ocean shore when the tide was out and the wet sands usually under the water breathed shallowly in the open air.

And then the skies darkened with unexpected speed, and the wondrous land… went away. Sar no longer smelled ocean or tasted fruit—she found herself lying curled into a tight ball, dirty pavement against her cheek, a rank smell of refuse in the alley behind her, and the remnants of a strange man on her and in her, and… something else… the faint scent of something that she now recognized, and understood, and *wanted*. Dreamshare powder. Dreamshare juice. She made out, with difficulty, the shattered remains of the vial from which she had drunk her first taste of it not far from where she was lying.

For a while, she could not move. She closed her eyes, and they filled, and overflowed; and the tears ran down her cheeks and into the corner of her mouth and all she could taste was the salt of them, the salt of the clean ocean she had left behind and which she could probably never return to again. Not like this. Not unclean.

Not when she was aware of waking to a craving she was helpless to ignore—a craving for a return to that land where fish swam in the green sky and gems hung from branches like strange shining fruit.

But she was here for a reason. For a *reason*. She forced herself to sit up, smooth down her clothes, remember the face of a man other than the one who had taken her here in the alley. Iorn. *Iorn*. He was somewhere in this city. She would find him. She had to find him.

A woman fed her, almost a full day later, with something exotic that Sar did not recognize, the unfamiliar taste masking the scent and flavor underneath—and the Dreamshare in the food took her again, and this time she went to a different place altogether, sharing it with the woman who had offered her the food, a woman's hands on the secret places of her body, a woman's lips on hers. Sar had not been wearing the code earring that indicated that she had been seeking a female Dreamshare partner, but the other woman had worn two earrings and apparently didn't care that Sar might not have been willing. She thought, although she was far from sure, that there might have even been more than one woman—because there were more hands than there ought to have been, and more mouths, and she was in a place that burned with flames that were violet and green and gold and she danced between them like a demon child and where they touched they did not burn with pain but with an intense pleasure that made her dizzy with exquisite feelings she could not even begin to identify. Where the flames touched they left a fiery trail of sparkles in the same color that they had been, and soon she was dancing naked in bare feet upon glowing embers and she herself, her body, her limbs, her hair, were glowing with the shades of the fires she had taken within herself.

She was lost, then—the streets took her, and held her, and she went where the scent of the drug led her... or waited until it led others to her. Every time she returned to herself it was with more memories of light... and to a greater and deeper despair.

It was nearly three weeks later that she found Iorn.

She had stumbled out of the city on the morning after yet another Dreamshare encounter, following a potholed and weed-infested street down towards the sea. It had finally taken her to a small half-moon of pebbly beach empty of people, its stones sharp and unsteady underneath her careful steps, hurting her feet. She only braved it because she suddenly craved the sensation of foam between her toes, of salt water flowing around her and cleansing her of the things that had wounded her, of the ocean's forgiveness of her sins and the gift of forgetting, if that was still possible.

She had not realized that she was not alone until she had waded waist-high into the water and stood with her torn skirts floating around her like a strange species of seaweed... and became aware that the shape at the ocean's edge to which she had only desultorily paid attention as she had made her way across the beach was in fact a man sitting hunched over with his legs drawn up against his body in the circle of his arms. It was not until the man moved ever so slightly, lifting his forehead from where it rested on his knees, that the sudden familiarity of the motion tore at her heart with a poisoned talon.

"Is that you?" she whispered, the words barely leaving her lips as sound.

He turned his head marginally to let his eyes slant sideways, just enough to glance at her, and then he lifted his head to look at her more fully, in astonishment.

"Sar...? Am I dreaming again? Are you real?"

"Real," she said. She drank him in, his face, the slope of his shoulders—his eyes were different than she remembered, wounded, quenched, and yes, still hungry, with a hunger she now understood. Shared. But he was still Iorn. Still hers. Her heart thudded painfully against her ribcage.

"What are you doing here?" he said, and the voice was harsh, bitter, stinging. He looked away, taking his eyes from her, and that hurt, hurt more than Sar knew it was possible to hurt. She had been willing to give so much for this moment, had paid what might have been too high a price already—and now, now that she was here and he was beside her, he would not look at her.

"I came to find you," she said, taking refuge in simple truth.

"Why?" he said, every word that came out of his mouth a dagger. "So you can see me crawl in the gutter? So you can come to reject me, or to gloat, or to preach?"

"No," Sar said simply.

She began to wade through the water towards him and he, realizing that she had done so, scrambled unsteadily to his feet.

"Don't come any closer," he said, an edge of desperation in his voice, panic blooming in his eyes. "I don't know that I can... I have already done so much that I..."

But she had reached him already, and stood beside him in silence for a moment, staring up at him, willing him to look at her again... and he finally did, reluctantly, as though his eyes had been dragged back to her face by main force of her will.

Both of them had eyes full of tears.

"It's too late," Iorn whispered hoarsely. "It's all over, it's far too late to do anything but mourn and seek another touch of Dream... you should not be here... you should never have come..."

The hunger was in her, too, stirred into a stabbing need at the very mention of the name of that thing that she craved. But the taste in her mouth was not sweet, it was salt, like the sea, like all the tears that she had shed.

She took one of Iorn's hands, folded it into a cup with her own small fingers curled on the outside, and then leaned forward to scoop up a handful of sea water with her other hand, letting it trickle and drip and dribble into his palm until hers was empty and she closed his own hand over it.

Clean water. Salt, like tears.

The sea forgave.

The hunger would always be there, but perhaps they could slake it with each other. Together. In a place far away from Ancirian-Shaba. In a place where memories did not burn, where they might never again find the magic lands where fish swam in water-colored skies but where they could, perhaps, in time, find peace.

"We can still share a life that is not this, a life that is not tainted. Let us go somewhere new, where nobody knows or remembers us, and start all over again." She spoke very softly, holding his eyes with her own, and then brought her fingers, still wet with salt water, and laid them against his lips. The taste of the sea. The taste of forgiveness. "We still have the future, you and I. It may not be the future that we have always been promised... but we have this day, and then the day after that, we can take it all a day at a time. That may be all that we have... but I will take it as it comes, from dawn to dawn, watching the tide come in, watching it go out. One day at a time. Perhaps we can get used to in, eventually, and learn to accept that it will remain real, and remain true. We *can*."

Sar smiled, suddenly, and it was like a shaft of sunlight waking a sparkle on the ocean.

"We can… we can share…Will you share a different dream with me… share the years to come…?"

She had not used the actual word, the name of the drug that owned them both, but she had skated close enough to it and Iorn recoiled. But Sar held on, her hand smaller and weaker than his own but its strength lying not in the power of its grip but in the power of its promise. And he finally sighed, letting the tenseness in his shoulders drain away. The sea whispered against the pebbled shore behind them; out towards the horizon, on the open ocean, the sun played on the water, sparkling and dancing amongst the waves. The sight of it was almost enough to sate the hunger that sat at the heart of them both now, the hunger that would always stalk them, that they could never feed again without the risk of being lost again, this time perhaps forever.

But the sea would be there for them. The salt and the sunlight.

It would have to be enough.

THE WORD BEHIND THE STORY

Ikigai (Japanese): a reason to get up in the morning, a reason to live

THE STORY BEHIND THE WORD

"Dreamshare" might have been written to illustrate this particular concept—the concept of how the answer to the question "What is life all about" can change as circumstances change, and the things that make you believe, that make you live, that literally make you get out of bed in the morning, shift and morph as the years go by and can be different from day to day. Except… that some things… stay. For my protagonist, Sar, the shining light of her lodestar was her unwavering devotion to the man she loved—her memory of him, and the substance of him. In the end, maybe, for him it was the same… after a detour chasing the fool's-gold glitter of something insubstantial and impermanent as exemplified in the visions brought by Dreamshare, the drug that stole him from Sar. Either way… a reason to live. Ikigai.

TROUVAILLE

THE BUCKET LIST

The first word I ever spoke was not Mama or Papa. It was, apparently, "Why?"

I have no memory of those early years, when curiosity was still young and unformed (and yet unquenchable) but the very earliest memories I do have, and trust as real, involved that question. I was three when I dismantled a clock because I wanted to know why it was able to measure time. I was seven when I first asked why some character from a kid's story book did as they did and not something else entirely. I was in high school when I drove a biology teacher nuts by wanting to know—at my first academic encounter with the concept—just *why*, and not *how*, evolution worked. I was in my early twenties when I wrecked what might have been my one-and-only soulmate romance by asking my then-partner so many times *why* she loved me that she began to question the reasons herself, and left.

You'd think I would have learned, but no. The question remained my core. I saw something, anything, and I wanted to know… well… *why*.

Which was probably the reason I slowed the car as I drove by a house with an unkempt yard and peeling paint, just off the side of a provincial back road in what passed for a 'town' (if only in the adjustment of the speed limits in what someone adorably considered a built-up area). The yard had a sign in it. The sign said, "3 for $10".

It was such an odd thing. Three what? Eggs? Second-hand science fiction paperbacks from the sixties? Red roses? Pieces of Lego? Children?

And then, fatally... *why* three for ten dollars?

I turned the car in the next driveway and cruised back to the house. Its yard was fenced, and gated, but the gate was hanging open by one hinge and didn't look as though it had been moved for an age. I had told myself I merely wanted another look, just in case I had managed to miss that detail that my *why*-mind now craved, but the sign was just as cryptic as I had thought it was, and it was curiosity that made me swing the car into that driveway and pull up in front of the house.

I switched off the engine and sat contemplating the building for a moment. It used to be some vibrant shade of blue or maybe green but that was weathered into a soft dove green gray where it wasn't flaking off the walls. The windows, one on either side of the front door, had once had white-painted frames but those were chipped down to bare wood, and the glass didn't look too clean. The front door itself had three concrete steps leading down into that yard, with its dandelion-starred un-mowed grass and a rusting metal barrel stood smack in the middle of that sad and neglected lawn, with that sign that had brought me here nailed to a wooden post stuck into the top of the barrel.

"3 for $10".

I considered the matter, and made a bargain with myself. If I had a $10 bill, itself, whole and self-identifying, I would go inside and pay it and see what I received in return. Not if I had to make it up with ones and fives or if I only had twenties which needed change. It was going to be easy, fated, or it wasn't going to happen at all.

There was only one note in my wallet when I opened it up.

A ten-dollar bill.

Well, okay then, I would find out why, after all.

If there was anyone here, in fact. The place looked curiously... abandoned.

Holding the money in my hand, I swung my legs out of the car and picked my way through the dandelions to the front door. There was no doorbell, so I simply knocked—three times, just because. At the final knock the door opened a crack and a pale blue eye peered through.

"Yasss?" said a creaky voice, which sounded as though it

didn't get nearly enough practice at speaking aloud.

I pointed at the sign. "I'm here for my three."

The door inched a little wider. "Well, so, you'd better come inside then."

I stepped into a narrow hallway, and then followed a hand gesture through another door on my right and into the front parlor. I could see my car through the dusty curtains on the window overlooking the driveway. The place was furnished sparingly, with a two-seater couch and an unrelated wingback armchair arranged haphazardly around a scuffed coffee table, a cabinet tucked against a far wall under one of those thrift-shop paintings that you just ached to put a dragon into just to make them of passing interest, all on a wooden-plank floor, uneven, unpolished, covered by a single throw rug that barely stretched to fitting underneath that coffee table.

My host was a lanky man of indeterminate age, with a long neck sticking almost incongruously from a collarbone which looked as though he had accidentally swallowed a wire coat hanger. His salt-and-pepper hair looked in need of a scrub, stringy with grease and brushing his narrow shoulders. He appeared to be waiting for something, and I experimentally waved the tenner in his direction. He blinked, and took it from me, almost gingerly, as though he expected it to bite him.

"In the back room," he said, pointing to another door.

"What is?"

"The bucket."

"The…bucket?" I echoed, nonplussed.

He nodded. "You'll know what to do."

Apparently that was all I was going to get, because he took a couple of small steps back and out of the parlor, back into the entrance corridor, closing the door behind him.

The questions were starting to buzz around my head like stirred up hornets. But I was here, and my ten dollars was accepted, and there was the bucket.

So, I opened the door to the back room.

I don't know that I expected to find it empty of everything *but* the bucket, but that's exactly what greeted me. An empty room, with the same old wooden plank floor as the front parlor, but this time without even a scrap or rug or carpet. No furniture. Nothing on the walls. Just this plain metal aluminium bucket, the cheap kind, the ones you could probably buy in any hardware store for less than those ten bucks I had just handed over to the weird guy with the long hair.

Beginning to think that I'd been had, I stepped closer, frowning, and examined the bucket. It was clean, and contained absolutely nothing. And it just stood there like some bizarre representational piece of art.

He said I'd know what to do but I was damned if I did. However, despite the impulse to turn and walk right out the way I had come in, those hornet-questions made me step closer and peer at the bucket. At first glance nothing at all distinguished it from any other bucket in existence... nothing... except...

There was a shiny bit. A bit that was shinier than all the other bits.

A bit that looked like it might have been...

...*rubbed.*

"Oh, you have to be kidding me," I muttered, staring at the offending receptacle.

Someone was trying to tell me that this was a genie lamp? A genie... bucket?

Which would give you three of... something... for ten dollars.

Three what? Three wishes? How? *Why* would any self-respecting genie reside in a cheap metal bucket? It wasn't even closed—how would something like that hold a spirit captive? Why a bucket...?

I really should have known better than to do anything arrantly stupid, but I watched my hand creep out and light gently on the edge of the bucket, my fingers curling down into a grip. I contemplated lifting the bucket, but did not; and then my fingertips inevitably inched forward towards the shiny bit. Closer. And closer. And then I watched my hand lift and the pads of my fingers rub on the shiny spot. Up and down. Very lightly.

Nothing happened. Nothing happened for a very long moment, a moment long enough to make me aware that I was holding my breath—and so I exhaled, slowly, and began to rise from my crouched position beside the bucket. And then froze as a voice behind me said,

"Well, then, what do you want?"

I whipped around, too fast, lost my balance, and ended up sprawled beside that damned bucket flat on my butt, legs sprawled in an ungainly tangle.

A man stood in the corner of the room, leaning against the wall, arms crossed over his chest, one leg crossed over the other at the ankle. He wore a wide brimmed hat from underneath of which two eyes glinted with what might have been amusement.

"Guh," I said, intelligently.

"We'll have to do better than that," he said. "I don't know what you've been told but I don't read minds."

I scrambled to my feet. Upright, we were of a height, he and I. But the hat… shadowed him in a weird way. I couldn't seem to make out his features. Nothing except those glittering eyes which seemed to watch me with avidity, with mockery, with… attitudes I could not quite put into words.

"So," he said. "Pick. Today we have three live penguins, three dragon eggs, three tickets to undisclosed locations, three fleas, three burned out light bulbs, or of course the traditional three wishes—but you know how those can be tricksy."

"Three penguins?" I echoed, bewildered.

"Is that what you're choosing?"

"No—I mean—what?"

"Three for ten," he said. "That *is* what you came in here for, didn't you?"

"I just wanted to find out why—"

"Yes, of course. But you paid your money. Your ten. And now you get three. So, what do you want? The penguins?"

"Why would I want three penguins?" I finally spluttered.

He shrugged. "Beats me," he said. "But that's what in the bucket today. The bucket list is what it is. Nobody ever knows what it is—least of all me—until someone pays that fee and walks in here. And you don't get to take all day. Pick. Do you want me to run through your choices again?"

"I need a minute," I said.

"Take it," he said generously. "But at the end of it I want an answer. And the minute starts now."

A minute is really a very short time, and that's without the added dimension of utter bewilderment. But I gave it my best shot—penguins? Three *fleas*? Three dragon eggs—really, now? And then, practically, although I couldn't believe that I was doing this at all, the thought that I could have all the burned out light bulbs I wanted back home, if I cared to collect them, so no to those. The tickets which might take me anywhere? But I wouldn't know where? That almost appealed. The hornet's nest of questions buzzed a little louder. But they buzzed louder than *that* when I thought about the wishes.

I couldn't help a quick grin—what had he called it? The bucket list? The *bucket list*? Really? Literally?

"I take it you've made a choice?"

"Wishes," I said, lifting my chin.

He sighed. "They *all* choose wishes," he said, almost petulantly. "You'd think that more people would pick a mystery trip. Or gold. Or three true loves in a lifetime."

I considered that last one. "That doesn't sound like much of a bargain," I said. "The true love one."

I didn't actually see it move but by the tone of his voice one of his eyebrows rose up into his hairline. "And how so?"

"Well, can't you only have one at a time? True love, I mean? And if that's the case then you'd have to lose two to get the third. Which means you'd have to have your heart broken twice. And how do you get to pick which is the last? What if it was one of the ones you lost whom you would have preferred to keep?"

"Tough customer," he said. "You're a picker of nits, are you."

"I just would want to know why…"

"Yes," he said. "You would. Well. Wishes, then. What's your first?"

I spoke without thinking. "Amanda."

"Done," he said.

He had really understood? It was that easy?

"I thought you couldn't read minds," I said.

"Not as a rule. But these are the wishes. You state a name, that has baggage. You want that person, the person you named, to be lucky, happy, healthy, wealthy, well. All the good things. Understood. So, done."

"But she's…"

"The cancer scare? Don't worry about it. Taken care of. I told you, done."

"That easy?"

There was a grin in his voice, from the under-brim shadows. "That easy. Next?"

I hesitated. For some reason, the image of my empty wallet swam into my mind, and I opened my mouth without thinking. "That I should always have…"

"Done," he said. "Go on, then, look."

I hauled out my wallet. In my hand it felt just as it always did, thin, flat, empty.

"Open it," he said.

I did. Inside, there was a single note. A crisp new ten dollar bill.

"But I just gave…" I began, pulling the money out and peering at it, reflexively closing the wallet with my other hand. "I know there wasn't…"

"Open it," he said again.

Fumbling with the note, I glanced up at him while opening up the wallet again.

Which had been empty, because I had taken out the ten dollars. Which I still held in my hand. But now there was another ten dollar bill inside the wallet, exactly like the first. I stared at the two notes, and then lifted my head, my jaw hanging open, and stared at the genie.

"Ten, because that is what you most recently wanted, needed, and used," he said. "From here on, when you open it, whatever you want, need, or find yourself in a position to have to pay at any given moment. Enough for the occasion. For that occasion. Enough to meet any immediate need expressed in dollar terms."

"If I wanted a cup of coffee…? If I wanted a new car? A new house?"

"All of those things," he said, sounding amused. "Don't lose that wallet."

"But is it real money?"

"Real?"

"I mean, does it stay… is the person I pay going to have… will it just…"

"Real enough for the purpose for which it was intended," he said, and now I knew he was laughing at me. "Whoever needs to be paid is paid and once they have the money it's real money. It won't turn into dry leaves and blow away as soon as you shake the dust of a place off your feet. But it's sweet that you care. Or are you afraid that some unsavory type might come after you when the cash you've handed over melts away overnight? Don't worry, you're safe. I'm not saying it's going to stay with the people you've paid forever but then no money ever does, wished or unwished. And once you've handed over what you need to hand over it's not your problem any more. Bills are paid. Always paid. In full."

I didn't know why that sounded vaguely ominous but it did. I put the wallet away, carefully, shaking my head.

"I wish I knew why…" I began, and then clamped my mouth closed, fast.

Too late.

He pushed away from the wall.

"Done," he said. "You will know it all."

"No but wait—I wasn't ready—"

"Three wishes," he said. "But we do get a chance to wriggle free of the chains. Oh, this, too, you will now know. But that doesn't matter. Because…"

My vision blurred for a moment, the room dissolving around me into a weird blue twilight-tinged gloom, and then everything steadied again… except… that I was now seeing it through…

I was leaning on the wall in the corner. My arms crossed over my chest. A wide brimmed hat over my eyes.

Across the room from me a man stood, grinning broadly. Sandy-haired, with wide-set blue eyes, his large white teeth gleaming from between thin, cruel-looking lips. His skin was pale, as you might have expected from someone who had spent… heaven alone knew how long… locked up in this room, the slave of that bucket.

"Here's the lowdown," he said easily. "You can always offer the three wishes, on top of whatever else you get to pull out of the bucket on any given day. If they choose any of that, you don't get to argue. Give the three for ten, and they go away. If they choose the wishes—and oh, so *many* do!—you aren't allowed to hint at what they're supposed to want. But the moment they make a mistake they're yours, and you get to be free again. Until then... you get to be here. Handing out the prizes. Watching over the bucket list. Have fun. Oh, you won't need the wallet any more..." Somehow, it was in his hand. My wallet. My magic wallet with its never-ending supply of money.

I heard a groan and by his widening grin I knew it had been me that had made that sound. And then something else occurred to me and I stepped away from the wall towards him, my hands curling into fists.

He didn't react, didn't flinch, maybe he just grinned even harder.

"I know," he said, "but there's nothing you can do about it. I'll find her, don't worry, and I'll console her. You wished her happy. She will be. Oh, she *will* be." He gave me a sardonic half-salute, and turned towards the door. "The keeper will be in to see you shortly. They always come when you're new. There's stories about the world they've not heard lately. You earn your keep with those, for a while. They'll make an effort to bring in the rubes, and you'll have your chances. But you're too raw and too untutored to succeed at once and by the time you get to know what you're doing... before you know it... it's been years. Or centuries. Good luck, then. Have fun. Not everyone gets to be a genie, you know. But you might say... it could be on someone's... *bucket list.*" His grin was so wide that his face was almost splitting apart. "So long, friend. Thanks. You picked good wishes for your legacy to me—that isn't always true. You should see what a dog's breakfast I made of mine."

"How long..." I began, and my voice cracked a little. "How long have you been here?"

"Me? Not that long, I don't think. I'm a quick study. Not more than twenty years, I reckon. It should be okay. The guy before me...? Well, he was a different sort. Or maybe after a little

while you don't get to care so much any more and you get freed
by accident, by happening on the kind of young fool that I was.
That you were. But my predecessor... I don't know... I heard
screaming, outside the room, when he left. It might really have
been centuries."

He was opening the door and the room was already closing
in on me, dissolving me, driving me into the walls, the bare
floor... the bucket. I caught a glimpse of the parlor, of the
armchair, of the dusty curtains, but the world beyond was
already out of my reach.

The door closed. And there was darkness.

In the darkness, there were answers. All the answers I could
have dreamed of. But I no longer wanted to know why.

Just *when*. And *how*.

And I had all the time in the world to lay bitter plans about
the time to come—soon, now, ah, soon—when I could use the
vestiges of my own curiosity to make someone wish they knew
why. And I would find him. I would find him. And the bill for
the bucket list would come due.

THE WORD BEHIND THE STORY

Trouvaille (French): a valuable discovery or a lucky find—something lovely discovered by chance

THE STORY BEHIND THE WORD

Well, *technically*, this may not be something "lovely"—but you have to admit that finding a sign like this, leading to a room like this, would definitely fall under that definition. The word also implies something that is found almost by accident, unsought, and a random sign in a random yard on a random road one is on for random reasons… definitely qualifies as a "find", as something tripped over and picked up to be more closely examined. Sometimes if you stop to take too close a look at a "trouvaille" it may not provide exactly the rewards you might anticipate. Found things are exactly that—found—and they have to be taken as they are. They are unsought, they come unlooked-for, and they have to be accepted on their own terms. And dealt with as best can be.

MAMIHLAPINATAPEI

EQUINOX

They left when the first hint of chill touched the breeze from the lake, the summer people. The small cluster of tiny cottages that clung to the hillside just above the shingle beach emptied almost overnight, as though the summer people were worried that the first brush of cold air which hinted of a season that was not filled with warmth and languor would be enough to freeze them, and then to shatter them.

They packed up and went, and for a while there was movement and commotion and milling about and suitcases and people calling out their goodbyes to others who were slower in the process of taking their own leave. And then there was silence, louder and louder. Nothing but the lapping of the water on the shingle shore, and the wind in the trees.

By the time the winter people came, there was nobody left to see them.

The summer people never knew about the winter people. The winter people knew about the summer people, but never crossed their paths. When the veil was thinnest—at the Equinoxes, when the hours of light and dark balanced precisely— the winter folk and the summer folk might have mingled and shared, walking in the same world, under the same skies. But usually when the change came, the cottages by the lakes were empty and abandoned—one season's denizens having left, the others not yet arrived. It was just easier for each to ignore the other, or to pretend that they never even knew the other existed.

They should never have even glimpsed one another.

Except that they did.

There was the time when a summer girl turned back as she was leaving, for a last look at the place she was leaving behind… and saw the winter cottage instead, accidentally, just a glimpse, and the winter boy standing before it.

Their eyes met, locked. And then the world rushed between again, and they vanished from each other's sight.

Vivi was fifteen that summer. By the time she arrived home from her summer holiday, and stepped into the traces where she had left her 'real' life behind, picking up the normal everyday problems of school and boys and books and bickering parents and growing up, she had almost forgotten what she had seen at the lake cottage. *Almost.* But every now and then she'd catch herself drawing him, doodling him, the boy she had seen standing at the door of the cottage which her father had just locked as the family had left it, stuffing the key into his pocket, proprietorially, as though he owned the place… which he did.

Except that he did not. The eyes of the boy Vivi had seen told her otherwise. Her family was permitted access to the house during those few bright weeks of summer. The rest of the time… what happened there the rest of the time?

Who slept in Vivi's narrow bed with its blue-and-white bedspread when she wasn't there?

The question began to obsess her, as the months slid by into cold and Christmas. Everything she saw around her, everything she did, she found herself wondering if *he* saw and knew too. Who was he, that stranger? Was he even real? She had asked her mother about the cottage, at some point, looking up from a book she was barely concentrating on, curled up in an armchair before the electric fire.

"Who lives in the cottages when we aren't there?" her mother had echoed, repeating the question back at her in a bewildered tone of voice. "Nobody does, Vivi. They're summer cottages. We go there for the holidays, and while we aren't there… nobody *lives* there, darling. It isn't the sort of place you *live* in. Not permanently."

"But I saw…"

"You saw what, Vivi?"

"Nothing," Vivi said, turning back to her book. "Nobody."
She wondered if he could speak. What his voice sounded
like. She found herself listening for cadences of that imagined
voice when the boys in her class at school spoke and clamored,
trying to find a trace of him in there, the boy from the lake,
but she couldn't. At the same time she thought he would sound
softer and gentler than the general screech and holler of the
school corridors—or harsher, like a crow, perhaps, or the scream
of the winter wind through branches empty of leaves.

She wondered what he would think of her voice. She found
herself speaking differently, modulating the loudness of her
voice or the roundness of her vowels for the ears of somebody
who might literally never hear her utter a word. If her parents
noticed the change, they said nothing about it. She gathered up
the drawings she had made, the sketches that had somehow
caught the curiosity and yearning in his eyes which might have
been twin to what had been in her own, and hid them away.
If anyone had seen them, and asked, she could not have given
a coherent answer as to where they had come from. And she
did not feel like explaining why she wanted to know about the
sound of the boy's voice.

He did not have a name yet. They didn't gain names until they
chose a task to do and proved they could do it, and then the
name of that task was bestowed upon them. He was the second
son of He Who Stops Pipes From Freezing and She Who Kept
Paint From Peeling, the younger brother of He Who Watches The
Windows. They were the Second House From The Shore Steps
family. That was their cottage. Their responsibility. They were
its winter people, its caretakers, its custodians. The doors that
were locked to keep other summer people out were no barrier to
the winter people who kept the house up in the winter months.

He had no specific task. Not yet. He drifted, helping out. It
would come, whenever it came, some winter, when he set his
hand to something that nobody else could or would do, and
then he would have a name, and status, and responsibilities.
But before that happened, he was still a ghost, something
that almost existed but not quite. He wondered if she had her

name yet, the golden girl from summer whose eyes he had so disconcertingly met as the family was leaving for the season, and if so what it was, what she was good at. What she did.

He knew which room was hers, he could see her eye, her hand, in a couple of pencil drawings that had been left stuck in the mirror frame. He could recognize the lake. But it was a different lake from the one that he knew, with leafed out trees, and with thick summer shadows he had never seen. He wondered what she would think of his own vision of that lake, if she would draw it like he could see it.

If she knew that it changed color, and texture, and context. If she was aware that it was colder, greyer, less splashed with bright splotches of swimming costumes, and summer hats, and watermelon devoured with summer greed (white teeth sinking into red juicy sweetness and tearing it from green rind on the shoreline…), and pistachio ice cream. If she could ever comprehend that other lake at all, or even believe in it.

He lay on her bed, every so often, trying to find her dreams. But they were cobwebs by then, flotsam of summer, impossible to reconstruct. He wondered if they would be able to understand one another. If they even spoke the same language.

He had been early, at the cottage, that year. Earlier than he had been supposed to be. The winter people were never meant to show while the summer people were still there. Not even as they were leaving. The time to arrive was well after the last car had left, leaving the cottages empty and completely abandoned in its wake. That was when the winter people were supposed to get about their work.

But he had broken the rules. He had been there as they had been in the process of departing.

They were not supposed to be able to perceive one another. Those were the rules. There was the tiny, tiny exception—the Equinox exception—that was supposed to be the only time when they did, when they could, cross each other's path, touch each other. But it had not been the Equinox when he arrived, when she left. It had been in the last gasp of August, just before September brought the Equinox in. The days were still long— summer days, *their* days. He had been uncalled for, unwanted, unexpected. Perhaps it was just that unexpectedness that tore the veil, just a little. Because for a moment—just for a moment—they had *both* been there.

And he knew that she knew it too. That she had seen him.

His family hadn't known that he had done this. He was never going to tell them if he could help it. It was a transgression—a big enough one that perhaps meant that he would never get a name at all. There had been winter people before who had simply... disappeared. Nobody knew where, or asked. But for the first time he thought he might have an understanding of how, of why, of where. That perhaps he had not been the only one of the winter people to have looked into the eyes of a summer girl, or a summer boy. And found there something that they could not bear to forget or to leave behind.

The lake was gray and silent that year. He spent a lot of time lingering at the water's edge, staring out across the lake towards a distant shore often obscured by sleeves of fog in the winter mornings, watching the resident ducks quack and flutter and seek shelter against the cold winds. He couldn't seem to find it in himself to take up any job in the winter upkeep that year, let alone a specific one to which he would devote his days. He would not get his name that season.

He had an awful feeling that his name was lost, adrift, floating somewhere in the shredded summer dreams of a summer girl's mind.

Vivi looked for him when they returned to the cottage the summer she turned sixteen. She looked for him as they arrived, scouring the shore, the woods, peering around the corners of her family's cottage, of other cottages. But he was nowhere.

The summer was as summer always was. They swam in the lake. They played summer games, and played summer music and danced on the shingle shore, they lit bonfires and sang while someone played the guitar. Vivi got kissed, but didn't like it much and tried to avoid the boy who had stolen that kiss while they were all there sitting around the fire. That was hard to do in that small clutch of cottages by the water. When she did the summer stuff they all did, the boy who had kissed her was somehow always underfoot with his annoying puppy-dog eyes and eager smile, as though that stolen kiss entitled him to a whole lot more. Vivi found herself instinctively wiping her lips with the back of her hand when she thought of him, and that wasn't a good sign. She also found herself touching her lips lightly with her fingertips when her thoughts strayed to the other boy, the one whom she had thought she had seen the year before.

She *thought* she had seen. She had almost convinced herself that she had dreamed the whole thing. And she might have done, had it not been for the extreme vividness of the memory. She found herself sketching him again, the expression in his eyes, the shock of hair above his narrow pale face. She felt as though his ghost was in her room at night, whispering to her in that voice she could not quite bring herself to fully bring to life. Whispering about the lake and the naked trees and the wind, the fog and the ducks, and curlews on the dark water. Of winter stars.

Lying there in her summer bedroom, with the summer nights beating their wings like moths against her windows, she could imagine this place in a different season. It didn't quite occur to her to specifically connect this curious sensation with her lack of enthusiasm for what had been her first kiss—something that, if she were to believe the common wisdom of her culture, she was supposed to carry the memory of always, warming herself at it during her old age when it brought back the way she had been when she had been young. But hers—her own first kiss in the summer she turned sixteen—she had already half-forgotten. She only remembered that she had not wanted it or asked for it. It was a memory of annoyance and impatience and resentment rather than something pleasant and treasured.

She drew a girl kissing the winter boy. She did not intend the girl to be herself, but she drew in her own hair, her own thin arms.

She did not think about it too much.

She dreamed about him, the last night of their summer, the last night at the cottage—and, on impulse, she left that last drawing behind when she finished cleaning out her room in preparation for departure, hidden underneath the bedspread of her bed. And, as though he had been summoned by that dream, when she looked back as their car was pulling away, she saw him again, standing where he had been standing the year before.

This time, when their eyes met and locked, he raised a hand. As though in greeting. Or a farewell. She found herself thinking about that, as they drove away, back in her own proper bed in the real home where their real lives unspooled. It was a moment where time stopped, like something preserved in amber. It was as though, in the moment of its ending, that particular summer would never quite go away.

The winter people had withdrawn in good time and in good order that year, and he was in their ranks—still nameless, but belonging to his kindred, and dutifully following when the spring Equinox arrived and they left the cottages for the summer people, according to the ancient contract. He Who Stops Pipes From Freezing and She Who Kept Paint From Peeling had finished their work for the season, He Who Watches The Windows had done his own work—only a couple of seasons old—in a manner that did his name proud. The younger brother had reached the end of their season still a drifter, still nameless. Herded away from the cottages by his mother and his brother while his father led the way. Their time was over. He turned and looked back, often—but she was not yet there, the summer girl. He wondered if he would ever see her again.

They kept to themselves as they always did, and waited for the moment of their return. The September Equinox, when the balance of the days changed again, when the longer nights allowed them to walk in the world, when the shorter days became colder, greyer, theirs. But he escaped, once again, and returned early—in August, as the summer people were leaving. It was not permitted, it was against the rules and against their law, and he did it in secret, clandestinely, with nothing except hope to balance the evil that would happen if he had been caught at it. But for the second time he was lucky—or perhaps it was just destiny—and he was there to watch them leave again.

And he sought her family, and he lingered as the last boxes were loaded, and he saw her turn and look, again, as she had done the first time. And this time, he lifted his hand, and he waved.

It might be all they ever had. But it was something. It was a connection.

The winter was a hard one, long, brittle, cold. The wind blew constantly. The birds grew hungry. The trees shivered in their slumber. The ground was solid underfoot, and ice clung to the edges of the lake where it met the frozen shingle. And his family went dutifully about their work, caring for the summer cottages in the off season, making sure all was well.

It was a while before he drifted into her bedroom. A while before he lay down on her bed. A while before he discovered the thing she had left behind under the bedspread.

She had signed it. He had a name for her now, and he tucked it away into the deepest part of him, the part which he shared with nobody.

Vivi.

They had names, the summer people—names, which belonged to themselves, names that did not describe what they were and what they did, names which were their own and stood untrammeled by any other context. She had a name. A *name*. He stared at the drawing and sounded it out, shaping it with his mouth, never saying it out loud. Vivi. Vivi. Vivi. If they walked the same stretch of lakeside shingle and they met halfway, he would know what to call her.

She would not.

For the first time in his life he felt the lack of a name as something real, something solid, as though he lacked an eye, or a hand. He could not be her equal, not if she could tell him her name and he could not reciprocate. But in his world the only way he could own a name would be to dive deeper into that world, to become more wholly, more completely, one of the winter people. And that would distance him from her, not bring him closer. If he owned a name it would be harder to slip away, as he had done. He might never see Vivi again.

And if he did not do this thing, if he stayed nameless… well, winter people had known that before. Some of them had not gained a name by a certain turning point in their lives and after that… they were gone. Not spoken of. Not remembered. How could they be, when they had no names? They were just not there anymore. As though they had never been.

He wondered if that happened with the summer people, if one of them could simply be erased from existence by the simple erasure of a name.

And whether the fact that he now knew hers meant that she could never vanish, because he was part of the anchor holding her here. And if he failed to gain a name and disappeared through it… if she would also vanish. Go with him, wherever it was that winter people went when they went away. And if they would both have names there, something they could call each other…

The winter was a hard one, long, brittle, cold, empty of joy and full of difficult choices. He tried to forget about things every so often by thinking about other things, doing other things. He found himself sweeping snow off the cottage, when it came—off the railings, off the stairs, off the roof. Compulsively, as though it offended him by being there.

And by the end of the season, as they prepared to depart again, his mother gave him a name.

He Who Sweeps Snow.

He was trapped now. Theirs.

He had once wanted a name, badly. Now that he owned one, he wept.

He wrote the name down, with a stub of pencil he found in the drawer of her desk, on the drawing she had left for him, and left it in the same place that she had done. It was a greeting. Or perhaps a farewell.

And he wrote one more thing, which was neither. It was, perhaps, an invitation.

The year she turned seventeen, Vivi had her last lakeside summer.

She found the drawing, when her family returned to the cottage. She found the strange thing written down underneath where she had signed her own name. She knew who had written it. For some reason the knowledge frightened her. Badly.

And the word below that—written in ungainly letters, as though the writer had never written anything down before—the single word which made no sense at all and yet which meant everything.

Equinox.

She pressed some of the wildflowers which grew in the dappled sunlight of the woods, stuck them in between the pages of one of her father's old law books (why it was in the summer cottage at all Vivi didn't even know because nobody had ever looked at it there, it was covered in a layer of dust when she first took it down) until they were dry and flat and fragile, and then slipped them between two sheets of paper and left them as she had done the drawing the year before, underneath the bedspread, as they left for the season. It was a summer gift, it spoke of sunshine and long warm days and cool lemonade and bare feet on cool shingles washed by the lake waters. It was a gift of identity. She signed it again, although this time it had not been her making, her drawing—but it was her gift, and a part of her, and she signed her name to it.

And—on impulse—wrote *Equinox* underneath that.

As though it was a password to a secret country.

She watched the cottage, when they left that summer, her head turned back, for as long as she could see it. But he was not there.

He Who Sweeps Snow found the flowers when the winter people came for the season. He hugged the paper on which the pressed flowers were lightly taped down, and smiled. He saw the word, his word, written down in her hand, and he thought he understood.

He lingered at the cottage long after his family had gone, that year. Right until the night of the Equinox, until the moment that he—by the rules, by the Law—*had* to leave. He waited, patiently, alone, on the steps which led to the cottage door, on the shore of the lake.

She did not come.

For some reason, that opened up a devastation in him

that he did not believe he was capable of. But he was He Who Sweeps Snow, and he swept the snow from her cottage every day, all winter long. He left a few dry leaves from the previous fall, miraculously preserved in shape and color, on her bed for her to find, maybe. He whispered the word *Equinox* over them, as though they could pass it on to her. But he had to leave long before her people came, and so it was that he didn't know that she hadn't come to the cottage that summer until he fought his own nature, now, and returned early to the lakeshore...only to find a different family leaving the cottage than the one he waited for and hoped to see. There was no Vivi.

He could not know what had happened to his leaves, to his offering. If someone hadn't simply tossed them without a second thought into a waste basket, or outside, somewhere where they would finally wither into dust.

The winter was a hard one, long, brittle, cold. Empty. He swept the snow out of duty, because that was who he was. He walked the beach on the Equinox. She did not come.

Vivi went to Paris in the summer that she turned eighteen. And then, the summer she turned nineteen, she went to a distant tropical island, on her honeymoon, having almost surprised herself by getting married—to a man who looked nothing at all like the boy from the summer cottage. And then, when she was twenty, she spent the summer at her husband's family's home, by a different lake. She had a son to cradle in her arms by the time the Equinox rolled around the following spring. When that boy was two years old, there was a sister.

Days passed. Months. Years.

She pressed flowers, for a hobby, she said. She kept them for a while, at least, until she pressed new ones to take the place of the old ones, inside the covers of one her father's old law books. And she felt fluttery, unsettled, uneasy, at changes of season. As though she had almost heard something, once, a whisper of a voice, and had not quite stopped to listen, and now it was just a ghost, a haunting, something she could not quite remember and could not quite shake.

It was pure accident that she returned to the lakeside

cottages—just once, arbitrarily, not even to the same cottage her family had owned back when she was a girl—in the summer that her son was seven, her daughter five. She brought them with her, and watched them carefully so that they did not get into trouble at the lakeshore. She found herself drawing again, something she had not done for many years—drawing a face familiar, yet only half remembered. And wondered why, in the midst of a summer holiday, she thought of snow.

She remembered, at last, as they were leaving, and she turned her head to look back.

He was not there. But her mind's eye saw him quite clearly, the curiosity in his gaze, the strangeness of his eyes. The raised arm, in greeting, or farewell.

She returned, alone, in September, on the day of the Equinox. She walked the empty shores of the lake to which the last vestiges of summer still clung. And she wept.

THE WORD BEHIND THE STORY

Mamihlapinatapei : (Yagan—indigenous language of Tierra del Fuego)— "The wordless, yet meaningful look shared by two people who both desire to initiate something but are both reluctant to start."

THE STORY BEHIND THE WORD

The Summer People and the Winter People had come to me before, as an idea. It wasn't until this particular 'story prompt' focused my attention on their potential, though, that they truly sharpened for me into a story. And the story seems to be an elegiac one, a story of things that never happened and never could have happened... but they might have... and it all hinged on that moment of a meeting of eyes across an unbridgeable chasm.

IN THIS MOMENT

MOKITA

TO REMEMBER RIOBARRE

The coffin is so small. So small.

No mother could look upon that casket and not weep for the pity of it. But it's more than that for me, now. It's not just that it is my baby lying in that pitiful box, made for a doll's burial.

It's the shape of it.

They didn't want me to see my son before they took him away from me. They took pains over that. But I saw, so help me, I saw—and the wings that hung limply from the back of my baby boy could not possibly fit in that narrow, shallow box they have laid him in. That box is too square and somber and commonplace to hold a dream.

I wondered if they laid the wings over him, inside, when they cut them from him. To keep him warm in the dark.

They didn't want me to know—but this is the third night I have not taken the pills before bedtime, and things are beginning to come back to me now. Things that they never wanted any of us to remember. Things that were judged best that we forgot… and yet, there's the pills, and there are our leaders and our doctors and our counselors, all of whom have to know what the rest of us are forbidden to remember. How many have seen my son, after I gave birth to him? How many have seen him that did not love him, could not have any interest in him other than chalking up yet another stillborn boy—how many, so that I, his mother, was denied even that consolation?

Boys were rare in our community. We were up to our necks in little girls, and therefore our marriage customs reflected those numbers. I myself was the fourth wife of a high-ranking politician—he had ten, in all. Of those ten women, seven were mothers—and there were only two boys in the twelve children of the household.

They were spoiled, of course, as all boys were. As my brother Cam was. He was the only boy in my father's household, and he was held more precious than sweet water, out here in the wilderness of ocean and the few small islands that we call home. My mother was also his mother; I was full sister to him, and proud of it.

Until the day that they came for him, and took him, and locked him up in that place up in the hills where the insane people live.

I went out to see him every so often, and I had to admit that he didn't look any different than before—but that was before he started talking, and after he was tucked away in that place, where none but his fellow madmen could hear him (and most were men, alas…), he spoke like a prophet.

"I remember it all," he would tell me. "Unto us the sky was given, in Riobarre. The sky, which was green like the shallow clear waters over the coral reef in the morning sun, the sky was ours and it was loud with the beat of our wings. We played up there in the wind and the clouds in the daytime, and flew amongst the familiar stars at night—ah, but here the stars are strange and unforgiving, and the winds do not call us home as they did in Riobarre."

He would fling out his arms, and there was a light in his eyes, and while I could hear his voice I could almost share his dream—but then he'd stop speaking and the rest of it would come back, the pity of this delusion, and the shame of it—the only boy of my father's blood, locked away in the asylum, never more to follow in his father's footsteps. Ah, but the disappointment was great in our house. My mother never recovered from the burden of it. She shriveled and shrank and hid her once beautiful and now haggard face in unwashed hair and dirty muslin veils so that none could see that the light had gone out in her eyes and that her features had set into lines of pain and of suffering, etched so deep that she looked thirty years older than her age.

And Cam had done this, with his talk of wings. Of remembering.

I had been thirteen, precocious, and deeply hurt by my brother's fall from his pedestal. I tried to make it up to my mother, who would have none of me, and to my father, who looked at me and saw the son he had lost and turned away. When they married me off, at sixteen, I was happy to leave that house. My mother killed herself not long after, threw herself off the headland onto sharp rocks below, and my husband made it clear to me that he was being very generous by keeping me on as a wife. But I kept on going to see Cam, sometimes stealing away in secret so that none knew that I went to that place, so that my husband would not be tainted by it—Cam was my brother, whatever his faults, whatever his sickness, whatever his sins, and even after our mother died of his ills I could not abandon him.

My husband was not happy with these visits. "You do know that he *chooses* to stay up there in that wilderness?" he demanded of me once, when I returned from the asylum. "He has but to say the word and he could take his place in society— and what a place it would be, with your father's house behind him—with wealth and power waiting to be taken, and him the only male heir. But he chooses not to do that."

"He is sick," I dared to argue, with my eyes downcast as became a submissive wife of my rank and station and tainted lineage. "He is sick, and surely he does not choose sickness over health?"

"If he would but take the medication that he refuses daily," my husband said frostily, "all would be well, and the delusions of these… memories that he has would go away, and he would be one of us again. But there you have it. They tried to force him to take his pills but he found ways to disobey; they tried persuading him, and he refused. He has used up his chances, and therefore he will stay in the place of madmen until the day he dies. And you, wife, had better not take too much of that on yourself. The scent of madness clings, and I will not have my house so marked. Do you understand me?"

"Yes, husband, I understand," I said, but I went back to see Cam again, with offerings of fruit and dried fish. He was my brother.

He knew me; he'd greet me by name, with a kiss and the sincere affection of a brother for a sister. But it would not be too long before he would start about Riobarre and the winged people in its skies—and then he would ask me, disconcertingly, whether I was still taking my pills like a good girl and whether my mind was still wiped of all memory of what my kind used to be.

We all took the pills. The little red pills. The pills that we had to take because this place where we lived and called home was in some ways hostile to our presence and lacked all the nutrients that our bodies required. The pity of people like Cam was that their delusions were based at least partly on fact—this place was not where our people originated, and we *did* come here from some other, now long lost, place where these pills had not been necessary because we had all that we required in our environment. But that place, as all sane people knew well, was not winged Riobarre—and the pills were a nutritional supplement, nothing more. We took them to survive in a strange land. They were the price we had to pay, the thing we had had to trade for our safety and security when we fled the dangers of our native land. And it was strange, but the dangers were so much legend by the time I came to think on them that they were vague and nebulous and not very specific—and yet they must have once been very real and very powerful, else our ancestors would never have fled but would have stayed to fight them.

And I knew all this, everything that the sane people knew, all about the pills and the reasons why I took them together with my fellow wives before we turned in for the night, every night. And yet, on the days that I returned home from the asylum in the hills, I would look on the pills, and I would wonder.

I never told my husband this. He would have forbidden me to see Cam again.

And then, miraculously, I was pregnant with my first child—and they said the baby was a boy. I was delirious with my joy, and my husband smiled upon me and lavished gifts on me, and my fellow wives swung from joy in the glory reflected from the future mother of a son to darkest jealousy and then back again, three times every hour. It was a giddy time, those early days of pregnancy, a time I remember now with as much emotional disconnect as I did the legends of dangers that had driven my people into exile.

I went to see Cam only once, after I was told that I was expecting, and the encounter was rich and strange.

"So," he had said, laying a strong brown hand over my swelling belly, "you are breeding. And did they tell you all that you need to know about the having of children?"

"They have told me it will be a son," I said proudly, my chin held high.

"Have a care," Cam said, his voice lowered. "Have a care, because they have not told you all they know. Have they already spoken to you of the pills?"

"They have said nothing of the pills," I said, suddenly uncomfortable—because I was lying. They had instructed me to start taking a pill and a half every night for the duration of my pregnancy—because of the drain that the baby would be on the nutrients in my system. But Cam would not have known that, could not have known that. Had no reason to know it.

"Oh, my sweet sister," he said lovingly, touching my hair with great tenderness. "I will pray that you will be safe in the days to come. The extra half-pill a night is to keep the dreams at bay because the unborn will insert their memories into your mind and thus strengthened your own might wake and override the pills that you would ordinarily take. Have a care, lest they poison you. They cannot let the wings return…"

"Oh, Cam," I murmured, with tears in my eyes.

"Riobarre," he whispered, "knew what to do with the winged ones. Here—here they would be nothing but danger. They would confirm the memories that they have worked so far to make everyone forget. And they cannot survive, not here, not in this thin air. Not the winged ones. Ah, my sister, be careful— for you are my sister and of my blood and the memory might carry strongly…"

I left him feeling unsettled and afraid, and I did not return. Four nights after that visit, still haunted by it, I took only one pill instead of the pill-and-a-half that was offered to me by the senior wife of the household.

And I dreamed, that night. I dreamed vivid dreams, and the people in them were golden-skinned and bright-eyed, and on their shoulders bright wings sprang and spread out and glowed in the orange sunlight as they flew for joy in the clouds, chasing each other across the arc of the heavens and laughing for the joy of it—except that I could not hear their laughter, the dream was vision only with no sound.

And I woke with my pillow wet with my tears.

And the next night I took the extra half-pill, because I didn't think I could bear to dream again. And my night was so empty and cold that I woke shivering and lay awake while around me the rest of the household slept, and watched the sun come forth in the morning. The next night was the same. And the night after that I did not take the half-pill again, and the dream was back, the winged people dancing in the sky, this time at night, with bright stars above them, stars that were strange to me and yet oh, so achingly familiar... but still there was no sound, just the light and fire and glory of wings in the starlight.

The next night I took no pill at all.

And I could hear them, then. A distant echo, to be sure, but a heart-piercing melody that spoke to my spirit and told me many things—and the most frightening thing of all was the realization that what we had all called Cam's insanity might be a true memory after all—and that somehow I was the one that was sick, that was being kept sick by the pills that I was taking, while he was free and sane and able to know who he was and who he had once been, things that were denied me.

And then the senior wife caught me palming the pill the night after, and pandemonium broke loose.

"You will never return to the hills again," my husband said furiously. "Your brother has tainted you with his madness and we will see what we can do about that—but it is unforgivable that you have endangered my son while you were pursuing your delusions. You will be kept in close confinement until you have given birth to him. And after, we shall see what can be done. As for the pills... if I have to hold you down myself you will take the pills as you have always done. The life of my son depends on that."

I didn't hear the laughter of the winged ones again. They upped my daily dosage to two pills, and I was sleepy and torpid during the days and often sleepless at night. It seemed to me in my drugged state that everyone looked at me with pity or contempt or, worse, clinical detachment—as though I was now no more than a womb for a boy child and of no further consequence myself.

They stood close around me on the night that my son was born, and it was hard to see—there was pain, and they gave me nothing to ease that although I felt my tissues tearing at his passage. It is possible, I guess, that I could have imagined everything that I glimpsed in that hour, but I don't think so, and I think that Cam could have told me almost everything about it had I thought to ask him, had I dared to ask him.

The boy that was born to me was golden-skinned, and there were wings, still wet from the fluids of his birth, hanging down from his shoulders as they took him from my womb and held him up. I heard him cry out, the cry of a living child, and then they closed in around me.

"He is stillborn," a doctor told me firmly. "We will give you something, to make you sleep."

"I want to see him," I protested weakly, but my husband, who was there, merely shook his head.

"The child is dead," he said. "There is no point. There is nothing to remember."

Later—was it hours, or days, or weeks later?—they made me get up and get dressed and come to the funeral of my child. The child in that casket that sits there and mocks me, so small, so *wrong*. So wrong for the winged golden boy that I gave birth to and that they never wanted me to hold in my memory.

Whatever they do to me after this, I have resolved to do this—no more pills shall pass my lips from this night on.

I owe it to my son, whom they took from me.

I owe it to him to know what he was, what he could have been.

I owe it to him, and to myself, and to my brother Cam locked away for so long among the madmen—I owe it to all of us, to finally sweep aside the fog of oblivion that they have tried to draw over my past, my heritage. I owe it to all of us to remember Riobarre.

THE WORD BEHIND THE STORY

Mokita (New Guinean) the truth everyone knows but nobody says. It's similar to the English phrase "there's an elephant in the room."

THE STORY BEHIND THE WORD

Believe it or not, I dreamed this entire thing. As a story. Literally. From beginning to end. Practically with the dialogue in place. Sometimes these things happen to me, a story comes by in the night and plants itself and basically grows from that seed during the night presenting me with the full flower of it in the morning, with a bow on top, like a gift. I've always been grateful for that. This particular story first saw publication in a magazine called "Time and Space", a handful of years ago, but its shape is so perfect for this particular word. Sometimes dream-gift stories just keep giving.

KOMOREBI

COLOR

He had come to give back what he had once begged for. To return the gift. To plead and grovel, if that was what it took, because it would mean a return to innocence.

"I cannot," she had said. "what I have given… cannot be taken away." She had reached out, traced a finger down the curve of his cheek, and then showed it to him, the fingertip damp with the tears that had streaked down his face when he had come into her presence. "This," she said. "I gave you this. You cannot unlearn to weep."

He remembered coming to this house—it wasn't as long ago as it now seemed to him, his days had been lengthened by his anguish. But the thing that had led him here, that had been building, for a while; it was as though he had been living on the edge of something for what seemed like several lifetimes, seeing something out of the corner of his eye, feeling a yearning he could not quite understand, overhearing conversations he could not make sense of.

Mahoud and Lila, it had been—the two human changelings— who had pushed him into it at last.

The humans stayed the age at which they had been taken, never growing older in the woods of Fae. Sometimes the reason why was obvious—the King or the Queen had a sudden hankering for nubile mortal flesh and they would turn up, the young knights or the girls barely stepping into the full flower of their womanhood, doomed to smile and to dance forever in the courts of the Fae, never to return to their homes and their families again even after the ones who had plucked them away from it all had long lost interest in them and had moved on to new favorites. But Fae could be random, or simply curious, or acting on geas, or occasionally just plain malicious. Sometimes the humans taken were older people, grandmothers snatched from hearthsides and condemned to an eternity of the aches and pains of old age or old men who hobbled through the woodland paths of the Fae kingdom with canes and walking sticks and used them, when taking a moment to rest from their exertions, to swat the nodding flower heads off their stems or to swipe at a passing doe, or dove, or butterfly.

And sometimes they were younger—much younger—than the ones chosen for reasons of physical infatuation alone. If they were babies, then the Fae allowed them to grow up—to a point—and then get stuck at whatever age the whim of the Fae had decreed. But if they were older than a handful of years—if taken at age five, or six, or seven—they would stay children of that age. The Fae didn't seem interested in allowing these to grow up and into young adults. After all, if the Fae wanted more young men and women there were more in the human kingdoms that were ripe for the taking, without waiting for the inconvenient years to pass until the children already underfoot grew up enough to become interesting.

Lila had been six years old when the Fae had stolen her away. She was a fragile pale child of sunny disposition and endless curiosity, and most of the Fae had time for her, to smile at her, to answer a question or two, to offer her the magic of a bird landing on her small wrist or a mushroom that tasted like gingerbread. But there were times when she was left to fend for herself, alone and lonely, and it was the other changelings who cared for her then.

Mahoud was thirteen human years old, but he had been living in the world of Fae for longer than anyone cared to remember. He was a thin, wiry, brown-skinned boy with skinny limbs and calloused bare feet; in his face, his dark eyes burned like twin coals. He was old enough to remember his world and what it was like and what it had meant—he had been a pauper born into a family of paupers who made their living thieving in the bazaars. Before Mahoud was seven he had been an accomplished cutpurse, contributing to the kitty of his large and tumbling family—his wizened father who was old before his time, worn down by a life of unrelenting hardship; his regretfully fecund mother, who could be counted on to produce a new baby almost every year; his tribe of brothers and sisters, nine of them by the time he had been snatched, ranging in age from babes in arms to grown men and to full-bodied women capable of bearing children of their own, and another in his mother's belly already.

Mahoud had been payment for an ill-conceived debt his father had been conned into owing one of the Jinni. That was pretty much all he knew of the matter—that, and the fact that one night he had gone to sleep as usual surrounded by people and noise and the smells of the dregs of the bazaar and the places where the poor people slept... and woken up here, in the woods of the Fae, in a place that was strange and foreign to him, stranger than anything he could have ever imagined. He had been frightened, in the beginning, and for a little while he had been cosseted by a number of the Fae who found him intriguing; if the Jinni who held his father's debt was one of these, Mahoud never knew it. But in time they drifted away, as Fae do, to other entertainments—and Mahoud had appointed himself the protector of the younger and more bewildered of the changeling children, as lost and adrift as he himself had once been.

Mahoud was Lila's guardian shadow, protecting her fiercely from harm or even a harsh word. The pair of them were always together, Mahoud's dark curly head bent down to her pale ringlets as they walked in the dappled translucent green light of sunlight filtered through pale green leaves of the trees in the Fae woods, or shared their meals by the brookside, or on the beach of the long lake where the water lapped gently at the shore. And he would keep her entertained, and stave off her sadness, by telling her stories, things he remembered from his own mortal days, things Lila had never seen or could barely imagine.

It was these that had drawn the attention—and eventually kindled an obsession—in the mind of a Fae who once overheard

Mahoud's stories purely by accident, and then found he could not stay away from that hypnotic voice and the images it conjured up.

"...busy paved courtyard," Mahoud would say, in his singsong voice and the exotic accent he had never lost, lying back against a piece of driftwood with Lila's small hand in his own and her head pillowed on his chest. "They sold herbs and potions and spices and incense over in the far corner, and you could tell, because the scents rose and mingled like spirits, and you could smell rose, and cinnamon, and patchouli, and cardamom and nutmeg, and sesame. And there would be honey sold in the stalls beside those, rich and fragrant and golden, and sesame cakes, and a man who roasted green berries right there in the market place filling the air with a heady aroma."

But Lila was a girl. "And the clothes?"

"Oh, the clothes," Mahoud said. "Over in the eastern quarter, they sold silks—scarlet silks, and sky blue, and golden, and even the most expensive of all, the purple, although it was supposed to be reserved for those in whose veins the blood ran royal... but you could buy it if you had enough gold, or you knew somebody, or you knew the right questions to ask. And next to that an old woman sold sheer veils in jewel hues, and next to her, the cobbler sat out in the streets and you could see how he made the shoes—the simple leather sandals for the poor folk, and the elaborate ones with long curved toes for the highborn ones in their halls of pale marble and porphyry and soft carpets."

"And the carpets?"

"You could buy them too, not far away, and behind them there were stalls which sold the skeins from which they were woven—the silk and the wool, dyed all the colors of the world."

"And what did the rich people buy?"

"They bought the best—they bought the carpets which they believed could fly, little girl—the most expensive ones of all, the ones woven from the finest wools, with intricate patterns of dark blue, and gold, and rose madder. And they bought hats and turbans out of golden silk, and jewelled hat pins with gems like blood-red rubies and sapphires, blue like a summer sky or the dark ones the color of midnight with bright stars swimming in their depths, jewels as big as your fist. And ropes of pearls, white like the teeth of maidens or flushed with a faint tinge of pink, like a dawn across the ocean, or pale blue, like the birds' eggs that they sold over in the part of the *souk* where the animals flapped and squawked and screamed and roared all together…"

"And what kind of animals?"

"Oh, all kinds! They sold monkeys with scarlet leather collars and leashes, and tawny lions captured far to the south, and blooded horses, midnight black or pure white or roan with four white socks. And also peacocks, with their magnificent tails and the plumes winking purple and green in the fall of blue feathers. And birds of paradise, red and white and golden and green and blue, and the lyre birds with the strange tails, and then also…"

"The tigers?" Lila murmured, growing sleepy, her long-lashed eyes fluttering closed against the silk of his vest.

"The tigers," Mahoud said, his voice slipping into a whisper that was a lullaby. "The great tigers with their black-and-orange striped fur, and their glowing jewelled eyes…"

Other times, Lila would be the one telling the story—describing in vivid and childlike detail the gardens she remembered from her days in the human world, where she had been left to kick her heels on the green lawns of her mother's garden, watched over by a yawning nursemaid drifting off into a quiet nap on a summer afternoon… a nap which had allowed Lila to be snatched away… and that was the point in the story where she would always falter, and look sad, and then speak no more until Mahoud cajoled her into a smile many hours later. But until she got there, she would describe the flowers that grew in the garden as though they were still growing in ghostly profusion all around her.

"Mama told me all the names and I could never remember which was which," she explained earnestly to Mahoud. "There were foxgloves, and hollyhocks, and daisies, and poppies, and bluebells and things that smelled good, like hyacinth or lily of the valley. Lily of the valley was always white, but the others, there was blue, dark blue, like nanny's stockings—and there was pink—and there was yellow—oh, those were my favorites, the yellow!—and there were red ones, too. And she grew roses, I remember those, and they could be any color at all, white like the lily of the valley… and they could be yellow too… or dark, dark, dark red…"

"Like the Queen's rubies," Mahoud said.

"Redder," Lila said staunchly.

Such were their conversations, and their memories. They would talk of silks or flowers, and it would all come back to color and hue. Or Mahoud would start talking about the sky and the sea and how the color of the sky could change the color of the sea— or Lila would start asking him if where he came from the sky was a different color in spring and in summer and he would explain patiently that what she would call 'spring' was not a season in his own country, and no snow fell in what she would call 'winter'. And the one who lingered in the woods just out of their sight would listen, and he found himself fiercely missing… something that he had never, before that moment, realized that he had lacked.

The Fae never noticed color. They never saw it. They saw shape, and form, and light; to them, the adornments they wore, the jewels that gleamed on their clothes or in their hair, were chosen not by virtue of their color but by how bright they were, and how the internal facets in their depths where the light was caught and broken and reflected back changed the quality of that light.

The one who listened to the two human children talk of color would rise from his place of hiding, and walk out on his own, and stare hard at the sky above his head or at the waters of the lake to see if he could glimpse what the children had been talking about. He began to spend his time painfully trying to compare the quality and—yes—the color of the light which broke into a summer's day, or wound down a winter twilight; he would sense that the quality of the light was different at different seasons or at different times of day or in the depths of the wood as compared to out in the middle of the lake, but he could only begin to glimpse it, to realize that there was something different, that it might have something to do with all that color that the children always talked about, the color of jewels and of living things and of the earth and the sky. But if he turned his head and took his focus away he saw again as the Fae saw, no more than that, no less—and no vivid colors to put hue and nuance into his world.

It was *not* his world.

But he could not let it go.

He even cornered Mahoud once, demanding that he explain the way he saw things, but only succeeded in frightening the boy and frustrating himself even further.

"It's no use," he said, throwing his hands up in resignation. "I don't understand."

"The witch in the garden of statues does," Mahoud said, after a small pause.

"What was that? How do you know?"

"Because I talked to her, and told her of things I had seen, and she could see it," Mahoud said.

"Why do you call her the witch?" The question was almost an afterthought, but the tone of Mahoud's voice had been one of respect, and awe, and not a little fear.

"They told me... when I first got here... that she had powers," Mahoud said, almost unwillingly, as though he was betraying a secret. "That she had walked in the human world. That she might be able to return a human child to the place from where he had been taken."

"I listened to your stories," the Fae said slowly, staring at the human boy. "Your life was not easy. But here, you are not hungry and you do not need to steal for your food—here, you have a place to sleep and no vermin nibble on you in the night—here, you have the freedom to go where you please and do what you wish..."

"And here, nobody loves me," Mahoud said softly.

The words fell into a silence. And then, after a long pause, after it became obvious that Mahoud had said everything that he had wanted to say, the Fae sighed.

"And could she help you?" he asked.

"She said that for those like me the road leads only in one direction," Mahoud said. "When I spoke to her she told me that most of the people I had known and loved would already be dust and ashes. She could not take me back, not to the moment in which the Jinni took me in place of my father's debt, not to the warmth of my mother's love, or my sisters' affection—and those were the things I wanted to go back *to*."

"Human emotion," the Fae said. "Ephemeral and passing."

"And eternal," Mahoud said. "*She* understands."

He had never thought of the one who dwelled in the garden of statues as a witch of any sort. She was Fae, like himself, and that was enough. But Mahoud's words lingered with him, and finally he found himself loitering on the path that led to her garden, the blind stone eyes of two of her statues staring unseeingly at him from either side of the carved wooden gate which stood ajar. If Lila had been there, she might have explained where all the flowers were supposed to go—but there were no flowers here, that the visitor could see, even though he glimpsed what might have been rose bushes allowed to go to twisted briar and tangling against the side of the house that stood there in the middle of the garden. The garden itself was a maze of paths, laid out in crumbled white stone or perhaps shell, winding their way like a labyrinth between green hedges, and statue after statue after statue brooding where the paths crossed and recrossed.

She had been waiting for him on her doorstep, the one he had come to see, leaning against the doorjamb, watching him approach slowly, almost unwillingly, but drawn to this place by something he could no longer hold down.

"I know why you have come," she had told him.

"I want to see," he said. "Never in my existence in this place have I thought of myself as blind—but I am, I *am*, and those children with their mortal eyes see the world far better and far brighter than me. I want to see the way they do. Just *once*, I want to see the way they do. To feel the colors on my skin."

"I can do this for you," she said. "Are you certain?"

"More certain than I have ever been of anything," he said, and he meant it. Then.

She lifted a small crystal phial, dangling it by the narrow neck between two fingers of her left hand. "This will open your eyes," she said. "A drop in each eye, that will be enough. I ask you again, are you sure?"

"I am," he said.

"Three times I must ask, and three times you must affirm it. Do you truly wish this to be done?"

"Yes," he said. "I wish it done."

"Kneel," she said, "and look up, and do not blink or close your eyes until I tell you to."

He did as he was bid, kneeling on the white path at her feet, feeling the sharp shards of whatever had been strewn upon it cut into his legs. She opened the phial and carefully allowed a single drop of the liquid within to fall into each eye. It burned, like acid, like fire, but she had told him to keep his eyes open and so he did it, concentrating on the points of pain on his knees and shins rather than on what his eyes had to endure. Only one small gasp of pain was permitted to escape.

It was she who reached out at last to fold his eyelids closed over the thing she had put into his eyes.

"It is done," she said. "Go, then, and see the things you wanted to see."

"And the price...?" he asked, after a moment, opening his eyes to stare at her.

"Oh, you will pay it," she said softly. "But not, perhaps, to me..."

He wandered for a while in the Fae woods, afterwards, feeling a little lost, a little afraid—but the obsession was upon him in full strength and power now, and he physically ached to experience that human sight that he had bought... for a price he still did not know the nature of.

And so he crossed the boundary, through the Shadowlands, into the world where the humans teemed and laughed and ran and loved and dreamed.

And for a little while, everything took his breath away. Everything was richer and brighter and more vivid than even Mahoud had managed to paint with his stories. He wandered the world that was open to him, from the *souks* and bazaars which still existed in the place where Mahoud's family had once walked, quite probably not greatly changed from his day—to the cottage gardens that little Lila had brought the memory of into the woods of the Fae—to rivers where light scintillated on the muddy brown waters and fishermen pulled out writhing fish from the deeps, impaled on cruel hooks and twisting iridescent in the sunshine—to the spread of wings of the scarab beetle, and the ladybird, and a kingfisher—to a bruise-colored sky brooding over a field of golden grain studded with scarlet heads of poppies—to the flower markets of the old cities, where tier upon tier of vibrant hues cascaded one upon another until his eyes hurt from the blaze of glory…

And then, slowly, he began to realize what he had done.

The colors were not just on the surface of things. They had roots deeper than that, sunk into the minds and souls of the creatures that his gaze touched, and he could see it all now. There was no hiding from any of it now. The veils had all been torn away, and the world was naked to him, and raw, and the colors had edges like sharp knives.

For every mysterious or serene blue, there was also a curling tendril of the blue of pain—of bruising, of enduring loss and sadness.

For every warm shade of yellow or gold, there was an amber-hued shadow lying on people's faces, huddling in the depths of their eyes—shadows of cowardice, or of malice.

For every green of leaf and bough that rested the eyes and healed the soul, there was a green wraith of envy and jealousy and possessive greed that lurked in the deep shadows of people's homes.

For every vivid scarlet and ruby red, there was an explosion of fury somewhere, tongues of flame—of anger and terror and cruelty, the fires that burned heretics, the fire that came out of the mouth of a gun, delivering death. '

For every color, there was a dark twin, a shadow, and it came to him in hues and nuances, just as he had dreamed, but he could not close his eyes to any of this, could not unsee, and when he tried… his eyes leaked, and burned with the same burning that he had felt when the witch from the garden of stone statues had put a drop from her phial into each of his trusting eyes.

He recoiled from it all, in the end—and ran back, to the things that he knew, to the quiet woods of the Fae. But the colors followed him there, the memory of it all, and it was as if they had lodged deep inside of him, a slow poison in his soul, and were never going to let him turn away again.

He endured—but before long they noticed, the others. He was the only one with eyes that ran water, and sometimes they would do that at a mere memory of something that he now carried within him. He began to avoid the other Fae, avoided the changelings altogether, drifted alone and wretched through the woods for a little while until he could take it no longer and made his unwilling way back to the garden of the statues and the witch who dwelled within.

To beg for it to be taken away.

Believing that it would be. Might be. Could be.

Right until the moment she shook her head and told him no.

"Mahoud said you understood—that you can see—if he speaks the truth then how do you bear it?"

"I ripped my own heart out and ate it dressed with saffron and cinnamon…but I would not do that to another… and it's already far too late for that, with you.," she said. "I could have offered you the same bargain, right at the beginning of it all, but, like all those who came here before you begging for the thing that you wanted, you would not have taken it, you would never have accepted the simple truth that the clarity of vision you demanded would shatter your own heart in your breast. For you… I only have three choices. I can take your eyes and leave you in darkness for ever more; I can take your memory and send you back into the world a drooling idiot who will spend his days wrestling with a regret and a sorrow that he knows no reason for; or I can turn you to stone and take it all, so you have neither soul nor memory and will feel nothing more ever again."

"What was in that phial?" he asked at last, his hands twisted into fists of fear, of fury, of shame.

"Tears," she said softly. "Human tears. And once you've

seen through human tears, you can never unsee that world again, gift and curse, yours to bear, now and until the end of time. Now choose—your eyes, your memory, or the stone."

In the end, it was no choice at all. His eyes, brimming with the human tears which she had put there, followed where she pointed—into her garden where all the paths led, where brooding statues lined the labyrinth. There was a place out there, waiting for another.

THE WORD BEHIND THE STORY

Komorebi (Japanese): the quality of dappled sunlight shining through trees—the interplay between the light and the leaves

THE STORY BEHIND THE WORD

I have always been aware of this word—of the idea behind it, of what it describes—to the point that I have specifically bemoaned the lack of a coherent description of precisely this, that inchoate filtered green light that comes down through the trees inside a forest on a bright sunny day. Days ago I drove down a tree-lined alley in this light—and knew and recognized it instantly—except this time I had the precise word for it at my fingertips. This story may not be directly pointed at the heart of the concept, but it is all about the truth in colors, and that seemed to be a solid fit for a story to illustrate this elusive but oh-so-familiar idea. There is a truth in every color. Even—perhaps especially—in a color you can't quite pin down. Like Komorebi.

MÅNGATA

GO THROUGH

It's a street. There are houses. They are old, built of brick, mortared, painted; the windows are framed in carved wood. There may be gargoyles on the edges of the roof—I don't know. I don't look up. I never look up.

At my feet, the cobbles—uneven, gray, worn. Sometimes wet with a persistent annoying drizzle, or with rain that has already come and gone leaving just puddles in its wake. Sometimes dry, dusty, absorbing sunlight, radiating heat back. I have to keep looking down as I walk because the street looks as though it might once have been a wave of water—a wave rising and falling, a memory of motion now caught and frozen for eternity under the old cobbles. If I don't look where I am going I will turn an ankle, twist a foot, stub a toe. There will be pain.

Pain. There is always pain. I think I carry it with me. I brought it here. I wear it. I leave it in the tracks I leave behind on the cobblestones.

Right until I fetch up once again at a door that should never have been in front of me.

That's the way I live my life. I stumble and stagger in the direction that I am perfectly certain I am supposed to be moving in—and then I find myself yet again in front of the unexpected door, the door I should never have met, never have touched, the door I should never ever ever even consider walking through—because I know where it goes, because

*I have no idea where it goes, because it is not a door that was meant
for me, but here I am and there it is and I open it and step through…*

She doesn't know, when she wakes, where she is. Not quite.
The bed—the room—they look vaguely familiar but she can't
be sure whether it's because she's seen this particular room
or slept in this particular bed before or because she's seen a
thousand rooms just like this one.

Beside her on the other pillow, he sleeps. He snores. There
is the shadow of a beard on his face. She tries to hunt through
her mind for his name, but fails. It's a man. That's all she knows.

She gets up, slowly, carefully, disturbing as little of the bed
as she can. She lays one long-fingered hand on the dusty curtain,
brings her face up close and inhales the musty scent of fabric
which hasn't been washed for years, puts her eye to the crack
where the two wings of the curtains have been pulled together,
peers outside. Nothing is quite familiar. Nothing is completely
strange. She almost thinks she recognizes the place. She is not
sure enough to swear to it. If she walked down this street and
turned a corner she is almost-but-not-quite-completely certain
that she would see an open square, with a tree whose outlines
she has known for years, with certain shops lining the square,
with a worn path through the grass where people persist in
taking shortcuts. But perhaps none of this is real. Perhaps she
has just dreamed it all, there in that bed which is still warm with
the memory of her presence—perhaps she has put together that
square in her mind from dozens of mental snapshots of places
she has known but it has never existed, in the shape or form that
she now visualizes it, outside the confines of her imagination.

She glances back to the bed. He is still asleep. She suddenly
knows that she could not bear it if he woke, if he looked up and
frowned as if he couldn't remember her face at all, or worse, if
he woke up and smiled and called her by name or called her his
darling. She can't face any of it. She's alone, here, now, in a cold
room with the grey light of early morning gathering outside
and the first shadowy shapes of scurrying people hugging the
houses, scuttling along the sidewalks with their heads down
and their shoulders hunched, their hands gloved and their

collars raised. That tree in that square which may or may not exist no longer has its leaves, she knows this for a certainty—it's autumn, late autumn, sliding into winter, the light tells her so.

She dresses in silence. There is a run in her pantyhose, draped across the back of the chair. No help for that. She slides her feet into the stockings, smoothes them over her legs. Pulls on a nondescript dark skirt, a sweater. There is a battered handbag lying by the door; she pads towards it in stocking feet, carrying a pair of sensible shoes in her left hand, picks up the handbag with the fingertips of her right hand—there is no other woman here, the bag must belong to her, after all. Somewhere, soon—not here, not now— perhaps over a cup of coffee in a cheap diner nearby—she's going to open the bag and rummage inside it, for identity, for something to tell her who she is, what she is doing here.

She hesitates at the door, shoes in one hand, bag in the other. It is not a door she remembers seeing before. But she remembers the fact that she has often hesitated before strange doors. That doors never quite lead where she expected them to. That she quite probably never meant to be in this unknown room in this unknown house on this unknown street with this unknown man in the bed—she was never meant to be here at all.

She doesn't know if she can leave—if she is able to leave. If, when she walks through the door, it will mean leaving life behind. But she knows nothing about what's on the other side of this door, just as she knows nothing at all about the things which she can see on this side of it, hesitating before it. She knows nothing at all. Nothing. So—stay or go—it matters very little.

She reaches out, with the edge of her hand holding the shoes. She pushes down the handle. The door opens, just a crack, silently. She doesn't look back as she slips through, into shadow. Behind her, the room sinks back into shadow, too.

It's a road. A dirt road. I've been on it forever, or perhaps I've only stepped on it moments ago. I don't know. I don't remember. Time is elastic, after all, bulging and distending, sometimes worn very thin, thin enough to lift up to your eye and look through and be able to glimpse other things on the far side as though you were looking through a fine chiffon scarf. But this... this is a road. It's dusty. There's nothing on either side of it but fields, empty ones. No cows. No horses. Not even hay bales. Just windblown fields, in between stands of trees. There are wire fences between the fields and the road—I'm not sure if they're to keep me off the fields or to keep the things that don't exist in those fields from stepping onto the road and gobbling me up.

There's a crossroads. It's just a place where four roads meet, in the shape of a geometric cross, a gigantic plus sign drawn on the landscape. There's a signpost, right there in the middle—it has signs, pointing in the four directions—but the signs have either worn down into illegibility or else they're in a different language altogether. I don't understand them.

Beside the signpost, there's a door. Just a door. A doorframe, with a closed door within. There's even a key in the lock—but it's just a door, and I can walk right around it, and it's a door from either side, leading absolutely nowhere at all. I am certain, utterly certain, that those travelers for whom the signpost is intelligible will never see this door at all—but for me, for those like me, there's always a door. A strange door which leads nowhere. A door that is an alternative to directions that are unknowable, and unknown—a part of the signpost, just as mysterious as all the rest. Every door opens into something. There are just too many doors that I should never even have seen, let alone passed through. Too many doors that lead from darkness into shadow, or into light too blinding to see. Doors that make me stumble. Doors that never allow me to pass them by, once I've seen them. Once seen, never unseen. Always there. A door ignored will return—again and again and again—until I reach for that key, for that handle, and crack it open. A door that should never have been in my path; a door without which my path would not exist.

She gets out of the car, slowly, her movements hinting at fatigue. She isn't sure how long she's been driving. She isn't sure where she started from, not any more. There is a large black and battered duffle bag in the back seat—as far as she knows, it's her only luggage. She has, in the moment she thinks of the bag, no idea as to what it contains—what items she had thought essential enough to carry, to bring with her, instead of leaving them behind… wherever it was that she had come from. Her toothbrush? Her childhood teddy bear? Her Bible? Her shotgun…?

Around her, darkness is beginning to rise, to seep into the sky from the black shadows underneath the trees ringing the parking lot—empty, except for her. There's a house looming just in front of her, a house with a sign illuminated by a single dim light, a sign that proclaims it to be an inn. It's a haven. A refuge. A place to rest for the night.

There's a light behind the drawn curtains of windows facing out to the parking lot. Somebody's home. But there's a door. And the door is closed.

She hesitates, before she knocks. The house feels like a stage set—a two-dimensional thing, no more, behind which lies the chaos of backstage—fake potted plants, and a cracked coffee cup, and a ratty moth-eaten sofa with the doilies from last year's production of *Arsenic and Old Lace* still draped on it, and a typewriter with no ribbon in it, and a bunch of dusty silk roses, and a stuffed dog, and half-painted wooden cutouts of trees and of people and of a fireplace with a painted fire which gives no warmth at all. If she passes through this door she might simply be stepping into all that fakery, living a life in which nothing is real at all. Or she might be stepping *from* that fake life into something warm and real and waiting—a world where that fireplace is real, and so is the fire, and she can curl up in the corner of the sofa with a real dog curled up at her feet and real coffee in the cup. All just waiting for her. Maybe the bag in the back of the car is empty—just a stage prop; maybe the car doesn't run at all. Maybe all of it at her back—the gathering twilight, the vehicle whose keys even now dangle from her fingers (ah, but are they real keys or fake…?) the mysterious piece of luggage supposedly belonging to her—all of that—perhaps all of it would simply vanish if she stepped through this door, as though none if it had ever been.

What a strange dream she's been having. Of lying, and

running, and hiding, and looking for sanctuary.

She should never have come here. Never have been on this empty and isolated road so late in the day. Never have known this inn existed. Never hesitated in front of its door.

She should never have seen this door in her life.

If she passes through, she will be a different person. She knows this. It frightens her.

It makes her happy.

She reaches for the door handle—if it opens to her touch, she decides, arbitrarily, on the spot, then she will walk through. If not, if it's locked and she has to ring or knock to ask for admittance, she will not stop here. She will drive on. Into the night.

Into the doorless night.

The door gives under her hand. Swings inwards. There's a light, somewhere, within.

Just as well. She knows, without knowing, that she would have come up against this door again, if she didn't choose it this time around. That's the way things are.

She steps through. She has already forgotten about the bag on the back seat of the car. Nothing it contains has anything to do with her, not any more. The future is behind a curtain; the past is a long-lost foreign country, almost forgotten.

It's a gate made of wrought iron.

It's a coal hatch

.

It's an airlock.

It's a gaping hole in the ground, only darkness within and beyond.

There are many doors.

They lead from memory into oblivion, from darkness to light, from warmth into icy cold, from dream into wakeful reality, from life into death and then back again.

I've seen many. Too many. So have you. We'll see more. They're portals, they're gates; they are inevitable, and they are everywhere, and there are some which you should never have seen or passed through at all… but you go where the waters of life wash you up, flotsam and jetsam, lapping at the steps leading from the sea up to the threshold of a door you don't recognize and yet always knew would be there. Doors are choices. They are wishes. They are sacrifices (oh yes, they are—look down at the old blood stains at your feet, traces of those who came here before you…)

They are passages.

I wear a key on a string around my neck. It fits any lock. You carry one too. We all do. We are latchkey kids, the grown-ups are away, we're home alone and must do the best we can. A door can lead home, or into frightening alien places you cannot ever hope to understand.

They are doors. Even the ones you should never have seen, never touched, never listened with your ear against the grain of the wood for the faint sounds of what might be stirring beyond—even those, even the ones you don't know, don't recognize, don't understand—especially those—they're yours. They're meant for you.

It's a street. It's a road. It's a sidewalk. It's an alley. It's a path between the stars… or the shining silver-sparkling path of moonlight reflected on an ocean, leading you towards the horizon.

Stop, and look. There's a door.

You'll never recognize it. You might.

Go through.

THE WORD BEHIND THE STORY

Mångata (Swedish): The word for the glimmering, roadlike reflection that the moon creates on water.

THE STORY BEHIND THE WORD

The inspiration behind this one came from the lyrics of a song I heard ONCE—just a few stray words that floated into my mind and would not let go—the concept of doors, passages, places you find because it is absolutely necessary to go through them to get to the far side where you actually need to be. It's a path laid out for you. And from there... it was an easy step to Mångata.

AWARE

LEAVING VIA CALLIA

The harbor was full of them that morning, big ships with sails like wings, sailors shouting and hefting big sacks of mysterious cargo down creaking gangplanks. Cloaked travelers disembarked gingerly down narrow walkways, stepping into closed carriages waiting to take them to some distant, rich destination. Ship captains, with plumed hats shading their faces and rapiers on their hips, swaggered into the town, looking for drinks and women.

"Someday," whispered the wide-eyed boy watching the ships bobbing at anchor, watching the captains depart. "Someday, that will be me…"

But someday was far away. Pico'Marco was seven years old. His life belonged to his family, and it consisted of chore upon chore—stables to muck out, courtyards to sweep, firewood to stack, the roast to turn, water to haul, chickens to feed, and drinks to serve in the common room. Thankfully it was his sisters' province to clean the rooms, scrub the floors, and fuss with baking bread.

All of that was still waiting—and the morning was half gone, and here he was, gawking at the ships again. At the dream. At the shimmering sea which he loved, so far out of reach. A ship's captain needed wealth, connections. A sea captain could never have been an innkeeper's brat with the rank smell of tobacco in his hair from serving ale in the smoky common room and the stain of beer and tobacco-colored spit on his britches.

Turning his back on the sun-gilded sea and the swaying masts of the great ships, the boy wiped the back of his hand against his eyes and started home. He would have to sneak back in, pretend he'd been there all morning, or there would be Mamma's wrath to face again. And the Talk—duty, and loyalty, and family obligations. He would have made it, too, had Blanco, the soot-smeared kitchen cat who had last been white when he was a week-old kitten, not decided to show his affection at precisely the wrong moment and tangled himself, purring loudly, into the boy's feet. The truant stumbled, barked his shin on the nearest bench, and was betrayed into a groan of pain.

"About time you showed up," Mamma said with asperity. "Ships again, Pico'Marco...? I should have known. Wait till your father hears of it."

"But, Mamma..."

"None of that. You've already skived your chores for the day. Now make yourself useful. Here's Nonno's lunch; you can go feed him."

Nonno had a seat in one of the courtyards, in the shade of a small gnarled tree that grew from a crack between two paving stones. He could be a pleasant, laughing old man who played games and told stories—but when he wasn't... Ah, when he wasn't, he was a harsh-voiced, demanding, drooling tyrant who didn't know and didn't care who was caring for him. He could curl his twisted fingers around a wrist with a death grip and pull a small boy right up close, nose to nose, while he spat out incomprehensible curses and the boy drowned in hot breath heavily flavored with the stench of rotten teeth. And you never knew which Nonno you would get—the gentle, kind grandfather who would tell you wonderful tales of travel and adventure or the nightmare creature of his senility.

Pico'Marco was lucky this time. He could tell as soon as he peered into the courtyard that Nonno was having one of his good days.

"Pico'Marco," Nonno said in greeting, his voice thin and almost transparent with age. "Come sit with me a while." He patted the bench beside him.

Pico'Marco crossed the court and perched obediently where Nonno pointed.

"Talk to me while I eat," said Nonno. "I sense you have had an adventure today."

"How do you know?" Pico'Marco said, as he lifted a spoonful of gruel to Nonno's lips.

"I heard your mother," Nonno mumbled around the spoon.

"I was in the harbor," Pico'Marco began, carefully feeding spoonfuls of gruel to the old man. "The ships, Nonno, the tall ships! I could see the brass shining, and there were all these people on the quay, and the captains wore scarlet feathers in their hats. And there were women…"

"You aren't supposed to notice the women," cackled Nonno lasciviously. A thin stream of gruel ran down the corner of his mouth. Pico'Marco wiped it with the edge of his sleeve.

"Someday, Nonno. Someday, that will be me on those ships. I've seen the things they bring from their voyages, the bright silks and the carved bone… and the spices, Nonno, I could smell the spices… someday I'll get out of here. I'll go far away, very far from Via Callia."

"Ship's captains need to know how to read and to cypher," Nonno said, his voice thick with gruel.

"I'll learn!"

There was a gleam of his malicious side in the old man's eye as he cocked his gaze down on his small grandson. "Hah!" he said. "You'll get out. I swore I would get out for years, boy, and look at me. I'll die here and you'll bury my bones and nobody will even remember I ever lived. I'll tell you how you'll know when you will get away from here," he said, dropping his voice into a sudden conspiratorial whisper. "You see this tree? It blossoms every spring, the poor thing, I don't know why because it's never borne any fruit that I know of. White flowers, delicate, like lace. Like lace… On the morning, my boy, that you see those flowers opening in the dawn light, that's the day you'll leave Via Callia."

"But… I've seen the flowers," Pico'Marco said.

"I said, when you see the flowers opening, not when you see the tree in bloom," said Nonno. "When you see the bud on the tree unfurl into the flower. I've watched that tree these many years and never once did I see the flowers open on that first morning. I would just wake, they were there on the bough, and it was another year of toil that lay ahead."

"Nonno…"

"I think I want to sleep, now," said the old man, slumping back and closing his eyes.

Pico'Marco beat a prudent retreat with the half-full bowl of gruel. Better to face Mamma's ire than one of Nonno's moods.

"Flowers," the old man whispered in a lost, yearning voice as Pico'Marco crept away. "White flowers in the dawn…"

The following year, after Pico'Marco had turned eight, he'd been loitering on his market errands, as usual. He didn't make it as far as the harbor this time. Something Nonno had said had stuck with him—'sea captains needed to be able to read and cypher'—and it was this that focused his attention on the craftsman sitting cross-legged at a low table, dipping a goose quill into an inkwell, producing long lines of flowing black script while a customer sat opposite him with an air of reverence. Pico'Marco watched, fascinated, as the scribe finished his task, blotted the parchment with sand, and then read back to the customer what he had written. This was to the customer's satisfaction. Several coins changed hands. The customer carefully rolled up his precious parchment and departed. The scribe busied himself topping up the ink in his inkwell, and then looked up with an arched eyebrow and a quizzical smile.

"Something you require of me, young man?" he asked.

"Teach me to write!"

It was unpremeditated, bursting out of Pico'Marco, surprising both of them. The scribe straightened, staring at the scruffy urchin before him.

"Lessons cost money," he said laconically.

"I'm going to be a sea captain," Pico'Marco said, horrified to feel hot tears springing into his eyes. "And sea captains need to know their letters."

"Well," said the scribe. He gave the boy a slow, appraising look. "Come back next week," he said after a pause. "We will talk about it then."

"*Thank* you!" breathed Pico'Marco, who had been fully expecting to be, at best, laughed at and at worst chased away with a horsewhip for his presumption. Without wanting to give the scribe a chance to go back on his decision, the boy turned and ran from the marketplace.

Mamma collared him as soon as he returned to the inn. "Pico'Marco! Where have you been? Do I have to set a guard on you? Go, wash up, your food's getting cold. And then you can go and fetch fresh water for the kitchen."

She whirled, busy, distracted, and was out of the courtyard before Pico'Marco had a chance to reply. He sighed and followed her. It was going to be just another long, weary day, in a string of them, all exactly alike, one following another…

The very next morning, the world was broken.

Their neighbor, the cobbler Caribal, came hurrying into the inn's common room in great excitement.

"Have you heard?" he demanded. "The Duca has refused to pay the toll to the Master of the Straits. The Master has threatened to refuse our ships passage. The Duca said we'll take what is ours by right. We're at war!"

Hot on his heels came others. The common room did a brisk trade, a better day of business than many of late, but the news got worse and worse as the day grew older. The war news was confirmed, and then rumors started. Winters were bad for wars, but come spring there would be need for an army. An army could be trained over winter. Men were wanted.

A few volunteered. It soon became apparent that the rest would be taken, with or without their consent.

A recruiting officer duly turned up at the inn, and ran a bony thumb down a list as a clutch of sullen-faced young men waited in grim silence behind him.

"We have a Garanno Vanni here," the officer said. "He is hereby ordered to accompany us to the barracks, to be trained as a foot soldier."

"He is only sixteen!" Mamma burst out.

"That is correct," said the officer implacably. "Do you want us to send grandfathers into battle, goodwife?"

"But he is a *child*, you can't send a child…"

"Well, if you have a volunteer to replace him, send him to the barracks before sundown tomorrow," snapped the officer.

"Come on, you rabble, it's high time you had some discipline drummed into you..."

Marco Vanni, Nonno's son, father to Garanno, to Pico'Marco and his twin Martino, to Sarina and Venella, was thirty nine years old that winter. The day after Garanno was taken, Marco went in to volunteer on his son's behalf. Neither of them returned. Mamma followed, the day after that, to find out what had happened, and was told that both her men had been taken away to a winter training camp for the Duca's new army. She came home, dry-eyed, her spine straight, and parcelled out the innkeeping chores between her remaining children. Pico'Marco's appointed day with the marketplace scribe came and went. He remembered his missed appointment almost two days after he was supposed to keep it; he crawled into the friendly concealing straw at the back of the stables and cried for an hour, alone. And then he shook the straw from his hair and straightened his britches and bent under the load again.

He saw the white flowers on the tree that spring, but he did not see them bloom, like Nonno had said. This would not be the year.

The Duca's war turned out to be a longer, bloodier, more bitter conflict than he could have guessed. It dragged on through the spring of that year, into the summer, into autumn. That winter a few men started straggling back home, some of them missing an eye or a limb. Nobody came home to Via Callia. The winter dragged on into another spring.

Late that summer, a stranger with one leg cut off at the knee stumbled into the common room at an inauspicious hour. Sarina, who had been scrubbing the floors at the time, glanced up, startled, as the bearded apparition lurched into the room.

"I'm sorry," she said, "but we're not open..."

"Don't you know me, child?" the visitor asked, voice cracked and tired, but nonetheless familiar.

"Pappa...?" Sarina whispered. "*Pappa*?"

Heedless of his filthy clothes, of the crutches only barely keeping him upright, she flung her arms around him, weeping uncontrollably. "Pappa! You're back! Mamma! Veni! *Mamma*! Pappa is back!"

He was, and he wasn't.

His body had returned, but his spirit was still out there on a distant battlefield where he had held his oldest son in his arms and watched him die. Marco Vanni came back to his inn and his family, but he spent his days brooding in some corner, drinking heavily, drowning his guilt at having survived the war that had claimed his child. If Pico'Marco had hoped that his father's return would lift the burden of the endless chores from his own shoulders, he was wrong.

The year that Pico'Marco turned thirteen, the family saw two funerals and a wedding. Pappa Marco had been fading, a little piece at a time, ever since he had returned, and one morning Mamma found him cold and dead in the bed beside her. He had barely been decently laid to rest when Nonno went into a steep decline. Very soon the old man could no longer sit in his chair underneath the courtyard tree. Pico'Marco was with him when he suddenly sat up in bed one morning, squinting at the doorway of his room, and said, "I am coming, Annina. I come…"

Pico'Marco turned, staring, but the room was empty except for the two of them. Nonno fell back on his pillow, his eyes filmed with white, his breath rattling in his throat. For a brief moment he returned to lucidity, recognizing his grandson.

"Pico…" he whispered. "The flowers…"

And then he was nothing, just a shell, his last breath leaving him like a gentle sigh, his hand falling from Pico'Marco's wrist.

"You are no longer Pico'Marco," Mamma said at Nonno's funeral. "Your Nonno was Marco, and so was your Pappa. But they are both dead and buried now. You are no longer 'little' Marco now. You're the only Marco I have left."

Being Mamma, she did not cry. But her voice broke, just a little. And Marco's heart broke with it, just a little. Because he knew that this was all the grief that Mamma would ever allow herself to show.

Two months after Nonno's funeral Venella, Marco's younger sister, was married. Her belly was already beginning to show when she stood up at her wedding; Mamma said nothing, but there was a slow humiliation in her eyes. This was flying in the face of everything Mamma had tried to instill into her children. But Veni seemed happy—smug, even—and could not wait to leave the inn and go off with her new husband.

Mamma taught the twins the rudiments of figuring, so that they could take over the day-to-day running of the inn. Martino seemed to take to the task with a great affinity. Marco still dreamed of ships—but there seemed to be fewer galleons now, after the war. His favorite, the *Vincienni*, was more warship than merchantman now, bristling with ports for the black-powder guns. It would take more than the ability to read and cypher to command a ship like that now.

The white flowers came and went with the season on the tree in the courtyard, and Marco noted their presence there every year in memory of Nonno—but he never saw them bloom, like Nonno had described. This was not the year.

Nor the next.

Nor the next.

Marco was very different to his twin, quieter, deeper. The boys had shared their hopes and dreams once, when they had been much younger, but they grew more and more distant as they grew older. Martino was aware of his brother's unvoiced yearning to escape Via Callia; it was written in Marco's face, in the sighs that escaped him when he thought nobody was watching, when his responsibilities did not sit on his shoulders, black and heavy like crows.

The boys were almost seventeen when, on a day like many another, they had been sitting at their book-keeping table in the back room beside a small window framing a corner of a crumbling tiled roof against a patch of open sky. Marco, his chin cupped in his palm, stared through it as though it bore the bars of a cage.

"Yes, the roof needs fixing," Martino had said abruptly.

"What?"

"I know," said Martino. "I want it too. I've always wanted it. But we are all that's left, I know. That changes nothing. I'll tell you what—we'll give each other a year, shall we? If you'll mind the home fires here, I'll go out and see the world. And then I'll come back. And then it will be your turn…"

Martino had his own reasons for bringing the subject up. Appealing to his brother's longing to escape would buy him the time that he needed to plan his own. Martino led a dangerous double life, of which his family knew nothing until Mamma found him gone one morning—complete with a large portion of the inn's savings in gold and an incoherent message left with the stable boy which consisted, according to the lad, of only a few terse sentences: *They are looking for me. I owe them a lot of money. Don't search for me. Farewell.*

Two thuggish men had come asking for him not long after. Not finding him, they left, threatening to kill him when they caught up with him.

In the summer of the year he turned eighteen, Marco met Annina, who shared the name of the grandmother whom he had never known. She was a year older than him, and considered 'difficult', with a reputation—she was not passive and biddable, as was expected of young girls, but a capable businesswoman who had been running her father's wine shop and the small family vineyard since she was fifteen. She had come to the inn to settle some wine sales and had dealt for the first time directly with Marco. He was quiet and gentle but possessed of a strength of character that appealed to the girl; her reputation as a headstrong shrew mattered little to him when weighed against the impact of vivid blue eyes and a cloud of wheaten hair.

There was something else, too. Annina was the only heiress to that small vineyard out in the hills. It wasn't the sea, but someday, maybe, there would be a place for Marco to go.

They were married before the year was out. That spring, waking beside his new wife, Marco noticed the white flowers already on the tree in the courtyard, and knew that this, again, was not the year he would leave Via Callia. But, for now, he was content.

Mamma died the year Marco's first child was born, a girl they called Vincienna. Annina had asked why he wanted to name the child thus, but he could not tell her that he was naming his daughter after the ship he would never command and so the name remained a mystery. Sarina, still unmarried, helped care for the child. The two women took over the day-to-day running of the inn with Marco shouldering the rest.

Before he was thirty his family had grown to four children. In the year that his youngest daughter was born he thought he had caught the flowers unfurling on the twisted old tree—but it had been a trick of the light. That same year Annina's wine shop, which she now ran in her own right since her father's death, had burned down; without its income to support the vineyard, it had had to be sold. On the day that the sale deed came through Marco had walked for a long time on the quays, staring at the ships which stood mocking him in the harbor.

Via Callia tightened its grip on him with every year.

Marco no longer waited for the white flowers on the courtyard tree. His children grew. Vincienna made a good marriage at seventeen, and had presented her father with his first grandchild, a boy she named after him, in the first year of her marriage. Sarina withered and died, and was buried in the family plot. Marco's grandson joined her there before he had turned two, dying of some childhood megrim that had no cure in their world. His mother had already been brought to childbed again with a set of twins, and there were new babies to care for—but none of them bore Marco's name, and he missed his sunny little namesake fiercely.

The winter of Marco's fifty-second year was harsh. Ice caught on the shallows of the sea for the first time in living memory, and trees cracked with the hard frosts with sounds like thunder. Annina caught a chill and started coughing at night, quietly, trying to muffle it against her bedcovers. Marco heard it and worried about it. He remembered Martino and the gold he had taken with him so many years before, and thought about how much firewood that gold would have bought for his family this bitter winter. But his brother had not been heard of since he had left the inn. His married sister, Venella, had moved to another town and had disappeared from his life. This was all he had left—this woman, their children, the children of those children. This was Via Callia.

On a morning with the scent of spring in the air Marco woke and sat up in bed, rubbing his eyes. The air was still chill but it had a promise of warmth to it, a harbinger of change, of better times. He slipped out of bed where Annina still slept, pale and exhausted, and padded out into the courtyard. It was early—dawn was only just beginning to paint the eastern sky a pale pink streaked with gold. A nightingale was finishing up the night's song and other birds, the morning chorus, were starting to pick up where he had left off. The cobbles of the court were slick with dew, but it was no longer frozen. And in the far corner…

Marco stopped, open-mouthed, staring. He had almost forgotten, but now his Nonno's words slipped back into his mind: *White flowers, delicate, like lace. Like lace… On the morning that you see those flowers opening in the dawn light, that's the day you'll leave Via Callia…*

And there they were, on that twisted, ancient old tree that had survived everything, even the bitter frosts of this unforgiving winter. Unfurling like the promise of spring. Like lace. White flowers, delicate, opening in the dawn.

"Annina!" Marco called, entranced, anxious not to disturb the beauty that was unfolding before him. "Annina, come, quickly, quickly….!"

"Oh, Marco…" he heard Annina's voice, very soft, but not filled with wonder—filled, instead, with a strange, bone-deep, unutterable grief.

He turned, saw her kneeling, her red, work-worn hands clasped gently around the hand of…

His hand.

He was lying there beside her in the tumbled coverlets of their bed. His eyes closed. His face pale, pale… white, like the flowers trembling in the dawn.

THE WORD BEHIND THE STORY

Aware (Japanese): the bittersweetness of a brief and fading moment of transcendent beauty

THE STORY BEHIND THE WORD

This is one of those words which, just seen on the page like this, looks a lot—too much—like an already familiar and completely unrelated English word. We all know what "Aware" means. In English. But in this incarnation—pronounced differently, and flowering in a different context, a different mindset—it is a beautiful thing. And this particular story is perfect for illustrating this new and poignant meaning of Aware.

INSHALLAH

NIGHT TRAIN

I remember the night I saw the ghost god.

It was late fall, and I remember stamping my feet on the damp wind-blown platform, tugging the collar of my coat higher around my neck and pulling a pretty but wholly inadequate hat down about my ears. My skirt twisted about my legs in the wind; my calves were open to the bite of the cold air. I could see my breath come out in pearly clouds against the dim yellow sodium lights as I breathed into my chilled, gloveless hands, peering down the track, hopeful that I would glimpse the lights of the train approaching behind the leafless trees.

The train was late, and day was quickly turning into night. And night trains had always been haunted… by a quiet sadness, by hopelessness, and occasionally by wraiths on the way to nowhere.

Mostly it happens on the midnight trains, the ones that run near-empty in the darkness. If any real humans are still awake and desperate enough to travel at this hour—if any real humans are driven to ride the empty trains while everyone else is asleep in their beds—these are the kind of people who know the unspoken rules, who know when to look away, when to pretend they have seen nothing, when not to acknowledge that for a little while they have been seeing the outlines of a seat through the body of the person next to them… until, finally, they realize that the seat is empty, the shell that occupied it gone as though it never was.

But it had been there; something had been there.

If you look, sometimes you can see them, riding the trains. Whether it's in the peak-hour traffic, when they are trying to get lost in the crowds, or in the half-empty carriages in the quiet times when passengers are few, the trains run in twilight and sickly yellow lights flicker wanly in the railroad cars.

Those other passengers—the flesh-and-blood ones—they sort of see the ghosts… and they sort of pretend not to. The ghosts may well be the reason that nobody ever meets another's eyes in these trains, that everyone is sitting tight and compact and trying to defend the tiny little sphere of private space which they carry wrapped around themselves. Sometimes you can catch a stray gaze as it rests for a moment on some random person sitting next to them—and then you can see that gaze flicker away, as though trapped in an indecent act. They look away, at a cell phone screen, at something rushing past the windows, at their feet, at their hands with fingers twisting together in their laps and twitching for something to occupy them.

They used to be Gods, those ghosts.

They know one another, on the trains—they're all avatars. This may not be the only incarnation in which they're drifting through the physical world, there may be others, twins or vastly differently imagined, impressed into the fabric of reality by the weight of faith alone. Somewhere around the place where they manifest there are hundreds or thousands, or perhaps just dozens, of flesh-and-blood people who know them and believe in them and remember them.

The ghost-gods are bitterly aware of how ephemeral they are for all the power they have once held—aware that they wander this sphere only so long as someone, somewhere, still believes. It is faith alone that sustains them, sitting by murky commuter train windows, brooding at tenements and abandoned warehouses and late-autumn trees from which all the leaves are finally gone. They may not know one another precisely, not by name—some of them are truly obscure and barely holding on, with only just enough substance not to be truly transparent.

But they know what they are when they cross paths with one another, and they'll acknowledge each other, very lightly, almost too subtly for anyone else to notice at all. *Yes. I can see you. I know you are still believed in. I can see you exist.*

And every now and then they would carefully *not* acknowledge something—seeing one of their kind fade… and die.

It was easy enough to do, un-seeing the death of someone else's gods.

It was very different… on the night I looked sideways and recognized a god of my own making. And he looked back.

The train had been late, more than fifteen minutes late, and I had been pretty much frozen by the time it arrived. Perhaps it was this. Perhaps it was simply the fact that I was *slowed*, that the ice had thickened in my blood and my perceptions, and that every eye movement I made was made with a ponderous heaviness—a gaze which slid across everything in slow motion and took in, perforce, more detail than it usually might have done because it lingered on objects, and on people, a fraction longer than would have been permitted if the usual rules had been observed.

I knew him, of course, the moment I saw him. He was sitting kitty-corner from me, in a seat which had a faded 'RESERVED FOR DISABLED PASSENGERS' sign peeling gently off the grimy wall at his back. There was a certain amount of delicious irony in this—he was obviously, in the avatar that he manifested in, anything but disabled… but he was a god on his way out and how much more disabled can you get than that? But that didn't come until later, that thought. The first thing that came to me in the wake of recognition was… something close to panic.

He did nothing, simply sat there in silence, holding my eyes.

The words roiled inside my own head, random and chaotic like a flock of startled starlings.

I know who you are…how… why are you…

"Yes," he said. Out loud.

In response to questions I had not been able to piece together into a coherent thought. *Yes. It is I. Once, you believed in me.*

Some gods are lonely gods, worshipped in silence and in solitude, shared with nobody—and he had been one of those.

I had not really imagined him, until now, until the moment I recognized him. He didn't even have a name. If I had tried to explain this to somebody in so many words I would have failed dismally to convey the things he had meant to me, but I think that many of us carry such personal gods within us—a sort of bodily equivalent of the *lares* or household gods of ancient Rome. A sort of… intimate portrait of all the things that we believe in, in an entity woven of things like pride, and luck, and grace, and love. It was the sort of god which simply said, *I believe in me.*

The trouble was, I no longer did. Not really. The "me" I had started out believing in, fresh out of school where I had been an academic star, had never emerged. All I ever salvaged from that were unfulfilled dreams, and shattered ideals. And the more I failed at the things I thought I was good at, the worse I became at the things that I had never been good at in the first place.

The reason I was on this train, alone, this night, was that I had just broken up—again—finally, this time I meant it, although it was the third time he had hit me and I had walked away from this, the latest loser in a long string of them. Failed relationships littered my past like mud puddles in the wake of a hard rain. I had waded determinedly into each and every one of those puddles, intent on finding a firm footing, on staying, this time, every new time, untainted by the muck and the stench of anything that had gone on before. I had never succeeded. And every time I failed, more of the mud and muck and filth clung to me and stained me. And the less I minded.

And here I was, alone again, nursing what would probably become a nice shiny set of bruises by dawn and quite possibly—quite probably—pregnant, which was what had caused the man whom I had told that he was about to become a father to raise a hand to me in the first place.

I was cold, and lonely, and utterly alone.

And my personal god had just reached the end of his rope.

"What happened?" he mouthed.

He was breaking the rules. The numina on the train never spoke to the mortals, never acknowledged their existence, in return for the same consideration. But he was not going to live through this night. He knew it. Gods would not be gods if they had not such self-awareness in them.

I could only shrug.

"I had dreams," I said. "You were one of them."

"I was all of them."

"Perhaps."

"There is an altar, you know. Still. In the back of your mind. To all of it—to *me*. It's all still there—the simple faith, the lamps that have grown cold through ignorance and despondence and fear." He sounded earnest. Intense. Desperate.

Determined to convince me to… to look back, to turn away from the dark, to think about all those dreams and ideals again.

But he was too late for that. Way too late. The reason those lamps were cold and dead was because I had already burned in them all the dreams and ideals I have ever had. Every shred of them. I was an empty shell, and there he was, my own personal god, fading before my eyes.

"I'm sorry," I said, after a moment. I was, genuinely. I was full to the brim with useless regrets, looking back over the wasted and fallow years, on all the potential that had never flowered, on all the dreams that had never been allowed to be born because I had been too afraid to stand by and watch them die. Better if I pretended that they had never existed at all than to let those butterflies out of their cocoons, one by one, and stand by helplessly while the weight of the world crushed the fragile wings before they'd ever had a chance to fully unfold. Better to pretend that they could never fly at all than to watch them try, and fail.

And so I had stopped believing

And here he was at last, my failure of faith, to put a face on it all.

He looked familiar—no reason why he should not, he was a product of my own mind, after all—but it was not the sort of familiarity that had one reaching to put a name to a face. It was more… a recognition of self, only buried behind a very different façade. Male to my female. Fair to my dark. Tall and broad-shouldered to my bird-boned slender. Perhaps that was a hint, right there, because he was built for strength, for quiet power, for a banked but fiery determination—all the things that I had somehow allowed myself to stop believing that I had, that I could own, that I could control.

But he was half-transparent now, I could see the shape of the seat back right through him. It was cracked blue vinyl; I could see the cracks, even more clearly than had he not been there at all. It was almost as though he had become a lens, focusing my eye on the things that he, while fully corporate and solid, had been concealing before.

"Don't do this," he said. "Don't give up." *Don't let me die.*

I felt as though I should cry, as though there should be a welling of tears at the waste of this, at the devastating prospect of a god dying. Of killing a god, slowly, as the faith drained and dripped away, drop by drop, leaving only a dark vacuum of space. But I was dry as an old bone, a fossil bleaching in the pitiless sun for the last million years.

He lost more of himself. The cracks in the vinyl at his back became livid through the wraith that remained.

"Don't," he said again. "Because of that which you carry."

He knew I was pregnant. Of course he knew. He was my own wilting spirit, in a way.

"And why would I have it?" I said at last. "Why would I bring life into this cold dark world?"

"It will be spring by the time it is here."

Dammit. This was *really* breaking the rules, but there was a third voice that now joined in. I turned my head marginally, and I thought I could guess which one she was. Vesna, possibly, the Slavic Goddess of Spring. Or perhaps Persephone. It was hard to tell, but she did sit there holding a blade of wheat in her hand, and there were petals in her hair, and she smelled of new grass and morning rain. The incongruity of it—the fact that here was a personal god about to vanish into the night while this creature, wholly mythological and anthropomorphic, was much more solid and corporeal—struck me forcefully; even drew a wry and appreciative smile from me, however fleeting.

"What's the likes of you doing in here?" I murmured. Well, the rules were shot, anyway.

"It is in the darkest winter," she said tranquilly, "that

spring *is* most passionately believed in."

Oh, good. She would sit and spout the catechism of her avatar at me, in between the good advice she was dishing out. I couldn't wait.

"She's right," said a fourth voice, behind me. I turned, flinging my elbow over the back of my seat, to look.

It was hard to guess. He was at once huge and elegantly proportioned, and improbably blond, and Nordic. Thor, maybe. Or, for that matter, Loki. It wouldn't surprise me in the least if the Trickster in some shape or form didn't weigh in on this.

For a moment, seen from a corner of my eye, I thought that my own godling had solidified a little, and looked a little more hopeful—but then his edges blurred again as I laughed.

"Spring is for those who wait for it," I said.

"Lots do," Thor, or Loki, said, gesturing at Vesna with one white hand. "Look at her. Look how solid she is. She is believed in. By many."

"I only need," said my godling softly, "to be believed in… by *one*."

I turned back to him. "I said… I was sorry. I truly do mean it. I'm… out of it. I'm just utterly and completely out of faith."

"You don't understand," Loki, or Thor, said. I turned back to glance at him and he was wearing something between a sincere smile and a definite knowing smirk.

"Of course I don't," I said. "I'm talking to a bunch of shadows…."

"Not what I'm talking about," Thor, or Loki, said. "You understand that perfectly, else you wouldn't be having this conversation at all. You would never have seen any of us—you'd be surprised how many never do. You understand *this* all too well—the train, and those whom you call shadows who travel on it to pass their eternities. But what you don't understand is that if *he* goes… you will follow. And you'll go into the same limbo. Dark shadow of lost faith, travelling the trains."

"You wouldn't," Vesna said quietly, "be the first."

"So? Where are they all?" I lifted my shoulders, stretched out my arms to encompass the rest of the carriage.

There were only a couple of other people in it—one, I figured, mortal and utterly human, dozing in his seat; one or maybe two more, ghost-gods whom I didn't recognize but whose identity, as non-mortals, I was perfectly certain of.

That's all I *thought* were in the carriage.

But once the Viking god and the Slavic goddess had said what they had said... I could suddenly see them all, *all* the shadows. All the lost souls. And that empty train was crowded, *packed*, with ghosts.

"But I thought..." I swung back to my godling. Still transparent, still staring at me with his soul... *my* soul... in his eyes.

"That we faded away when faith vanishes?" he questioned softly. "And you'd be right. But that's how it works for the ones who are not mortal. For the rest—for *you*—it works *the other way*. You stop believing in us and we fade from this train... and *you* take our place. All the extinguished faith in the universe... comes here to die. Or, perhaps, to live forever..."

I could not unsee them now, the ones crowding the empty train. They sat on the seats, sometimes three deep, not caring. The effect was disconcerting until I figured it out because that meant that several sets of features blurred together into a fuzzy whole which made no logical sense until one realized that they belonged to several different people. They stood in the aisles and the vestibules, filling them, holding on to the backs of the seats or clinging to grab bars, packed tight, individual legs and hips and elbows blending into each other's bodies. All silent, all tragic, with a dark quiet emptiness like the depths of interstellar space filling the void behind their vacant eyes.

"You," Loki, or Thor, said. "Look down at your feet. Not that long, maybe."

My ankle boots were black, scuffed with dust and dirt. At first glance I thought the patina of dirt was simply blending into the dirty linoleum floor beneath my feet. But when I looked closer I realized that it looked more as though they had sunk into the floor, that the boundary between the edge of my foot and the floor it was resting on was being quietly, softly, unobtrusively erased.

I heard a sharp intake of breath, and belatedly realized that it had been mine.

There had been many ways I had pictured myself leaving

this world. *This...* this living death... this had never been part of it. The prospect terrified me.

The problem was... it didn't terrify me back into believing. When I looked up again, I had proof of that. My godling had faded even further.

His eyes were translucent, which was disconcerting—he was looking straight at me but it didn't feel that way. It felt as though someone... something... was staring at me from beyond infinity.

"I'm sorry," he said.

The train intercom crackled into life, announcing the next station—and I suddenly wanted off, *needed* off, no matter what the station was. It didn't matter. Anywhere but here. Anywhere. I could find my way. I knew I could.

If only I could move...

It felt as though I was pulling my feet out of thick mud nearly sucking my boots right off my feet, but I dragged myself upright by main force of will, stood weaving for a moment while I found my balance, forced myself to take a step forward. Just as the train slowed to a stop and the doors began to whoosh open I managed to lurch forward, through the mass of ghosts in my way. They didn't seem to notice; I had my arms out in front of me to push my way through, to push them aside, instinctively, but of course there was nothing *to* push, just empty air, and I all but fell off the train, staggering onto the platform, losing my balance, going down on one knee, hard. My bag slid off my shoulder and hit the ground, spilling its contents in front of me. Half blind with fear and a wholly unexpected anguish, I could barely see the things it had scattered. I started to gather them up more by touch than by sight—but then, just as the train began to pull away, I looked up again and my blurred eyes presented me with a picture that was perfectly sharp and clear.

Faces, at the windows. Vesna, waving jauntily with her ear of wheat. Loki, or Thor, smiling a languid and inscrutable Norse smile as he gave me a slow nod.

And in the last window, smiling faintly, was a face both familiar and... different in a disconcerting way—a far more solid form of my godling than I had thought remained in that train.

"No," I whispered into the night. "No, I *don't* believe. I don't believe in you, not any more…"

The words formed in the air about my ears, like a whisper. *You no longer have to. That which you carry believes. We are all born believing..*

This… this was my daughter's god? The unborn child…? How was it even possible for something that was yet to acquire consciousness to have something as nebulous as faith?

My belly suddenly felt dark, and heavy. Just for a moment the potential life I carried inside of me felt less than something that should be treasured and nurtured and far more like a form of dark possession, something that had forced my own cowering spirit to live to believe. Or, perhaps, to believe in order to live… in order for that thing inside of me to live. If I rubbed out the last of my faith, there would be nothing left for my child to anchor to. So *she* believed… she believed already, in my place, instead of me… she took my place, because she had to, in order to survive…

You believe. At least you did. If you truly had not… you would be one of the wraiths now. You are not. Look at you. You are solid. You are real. You are true. You are cold.

He had been right, the godling. On all counts.

Particularly that last.

I shivered. Faith, restored…? By what—by sheer terror? What kind of a price was that?

Should I never set foot on a train again…?

Faith. Restored. Renewed.

If I was supposed to believe again, I told myself firmly as I staggered to my feet and at least cast about for the name of the station where I had washed up, then I believe this: it would get warmer, right now. It would not rain. I would recognize the name of the place I was at.

I straightened up, into an evening which suddenly tightened with a ring of cold so intense that it cut my breath into ice. It didn't rain—it started to snow, big white flakes drifting down.

The platform had a sign proclaiming it to be Platform 4, but no other useful information that I could immediately see.

And I laughed, suddenly, lightly, into the night. I was standing here giving the universe conditions, making demands, wanting empirical proof; it had all but thumbed its nose at me.

And it didn't matter. The weight of a world had lifted from my shoulders, oddly. The universe was perverse—that was all there was to it.

I could live with that.

I could even *believe* it.

If you look, you can see them, riding the trains. In the peak-hour rush traffic, trying to get lost in the crowds; in the half-empty trains that run at twilight.

And I'd never again be able to pretend that they were not there.

Next time I climbed into a commuter train, I would keep an eye out for a familiar face. That god that my child—with eyes still closed to the world which she was yet to come into—had just made me see, smiling at me from a night-train's window as it pulled out of the station.

The lamps were still dark on that altar in the back of my mind—but a single candle had been lit. It might not be enough—it might not be nearly enough—but it would have to do.

THE WORD BEHIND THE STORY

Inshallah (Arabic): While it can be translated literally as "if Allah wills," the meaning of this phrase differs depending on the speaker's tone of voice. It can be a genuine sentiment, such as when talking to an old friend and parting with "We'll meet again, inshallah," or it can be used as a way to tacitly imply you actually aren't planning to do something. An example would be if someone proposes a meeting at 4 p.m., and you know you won't be able to make it on time. You can say, "I'll see you at 4, inshallah," meaning that you'll only make it on time if Allah wills it to happen.

THE STORY BEHIND THE WORD

I remember writing this story, sitting in a hotel lobby in the ember hours of a convention I was at, in Westchester County, waiting for the shuttle to take me to the train which would take me to the City which would take me to bus which would take me to an airport which would take me home. I wrote the bones of the story in an hour—maybe less—and then honed it, on that train ride through New York state while approaching the city of New York. I do believe things I saw out of the windows of that train made their way into the story, creeping in and making themselves at home. I polished it up on the airplane, flying across the breadth of the country, back to the West Coast which was home. I sent it out to the editors of an anthology shortly thereafter. The anthology was "Dark Faith II: Invocations", and the story (inshallah!) found itself a home there. Gods are everywhere.

THE GIFTS OF THE PAST

WON

SHE WORE YELLOW

She wore Yellow.

Standing on the far edge of the mourners at the funeral of my favourite asshole, she flamed like a torch, the only touch of colour in the chiaroscuro of the grey and white and black of the raiment that clothed those around her.

One would think that her presence, that colour, would make people whisper, or stare, or isolate her into a little pocket as the others drew away from her before they were contaminated by her. One would be wrong. It seemed that nobody else even knew she was there, that nobody could see her except me—and that was intriguing in itself, because it could mean that I'd simply imagined her, something bright and cheerful in all this fake bereavement. Because that is was what it was—fake—oh, there were a handful of people there who might have loved Bruce Mallow because society demanded that they do so, not because of what he was but in spite of it. His parents were dead, but his sister Clare was there (in deep black, and even looked as though she might have shed a tear or two) and his two ex-wives, the tall willowy blonde one who had since remarried someone who was by all accounts Bruce's (more) evil twin—the woman was a glutton for punishment—and the stringy little brunette who had come before the blonde, the first wife, the one he had married out of school because she was pregnant. His son, their son, wasn't at the funeral at all. Perhaps he had managed to escape.

Afterwards, when it was all over and the black-clad throng had begun to drift away in ones and twos from the yawning grave, I saw several people actually pause by Yellow and shake her hand with expressions which almost fell into the realm of condolences. The idea of somebody actually needing an expression of condolences because Bruce Mallow was gone would have intrigued me even had she not worn such an... unusual... shade to his interment. But by the time I had decided that I wanted to make a better acquaintance with Yellow, she had turned and was walking briskly away—and running after her felt... well... unseemly. Bruce would probably have done it, even with both the wives watching—that's partly because he was an asshole. He didn't care what anybody thought about the things he did so long as he got the things he wanted when he wanted them.

He would have wanted Yellow. I watched her walking diagonally across the grass, zigzagging between other gravestones, and she was something, indeed—long legs, slim body upholstered in that close-fitting yellow dress, shoulder-length brunette hair that almost but not quite shaded into mahogany.

I had been looking directly at her—and yet I found myself unable to recall her exact features, the shape of her mouth, the shade of her eyes. She had laid her presence on us lightly, and had erased it without effort; if a police presence had taken all the mourners aside as they left Bruce's grave I had the oddest feeling that nobody would have recalled seeing her at all, even though she had worn yellow, even though some of them had spoken to her, shaken her hand. She had slipped behind a potent *I was never here* field, and to my chagrin I, who had always had an eye for a pretty woman, had to struggle to keep her in the back of my mind.

Bruce would have remembered. Bruce would have had her sipping an apple martini at the closest bar ten minutes after the funeral. Probably out of that yellow dress within a couple of hours. A day, tops. He was disgustingly good at this.

Yellow was a mystery, though.

I was going to do something about finding out more—somebody in that throng of non-mourners must know who she was, and I was almost certain I could remember who she had spoken to at the funeral. Or I could figure it out if I tried. Or, anyway, there were ways…

I forgot all about her.

Right until the moment I saw her again.

She wore Green.

I knew it was her, instantly, even though her hair was redder than I thought I remembered it, and maybe longer. But it was her, I was sure of it.

There she was, standing in the back of the auditorium at my nephew Luke's graduation, shining out like an emerald. It was almost impossible to believe that nobody else noticed her, stared at her, singled her out in any way at all—but it was exactly like at the funeral, there she was at the periphery, and a couple of people I knew even nodded and smiled at her and one or two even shook her hand but I was too far away to hear what was said between them. I asked Luke if he knew her and he said, "Know who?" and then for a moment I lost her, and couldn't find her at all despite that glowing green dress that she had on. A brave shade, one that couldn't be worn by many—you'd think it would be impossible to mislay her wearing that colour, even there in the crowd. But when I tried to point her out to Luke I couldn't see her anywhere. Of course the moment he lost interest and turned away there she was again, as green as green can be. For a moment, I swear she looked my way, and *winked* at me. And maybe the eyes were green, as green as the dress.

This time I really was going to find out who she was and why she turned up at the places I was at. But I couldn't even be sure of her hair colour any more, never mind anything else—and she seemed to have perfected the art of blending into the wallpaper, no matter what kind of vivid shade she chose to wear, as soon as it became too obvious that my attention was fixed.

But, again, I… forgot. It was as though she walked through my mind with ease, brushing away traces of her passing as one does one's tracks in the sand with a palm frond. There, and not there. There, and gone.

She wore Red.

That was after the accident, when they wheeled me into the hospital on a gurney, and sure, maybe I was a little high on the oxygen—but it was her, I swear it was her, wearing what might have been ruby red scrubs, vanishing though one of those swinging doors that only surgeons can mysteriously pass. I wanted to claw the oxygen mask from my face, call out, but I'd been banged up good and everything was a little fuzzy, to be sure. Maybe I could even have been wrong. At any rate, she was not there when I woke up after my surgery with my spleen missing and steel pins holding together my left ankle.

The accident? I was looking over at the sidewalk. I swear, I *swear*, I saw Bruce walking there with his arm around somebody who bore a strong resemblance to the blonde wife. The Bruce we had laid into the ground not that long before. Wouldn't you have driven into the car in front of you if you'd seen a dead man walking? Yeah, didn't think so. I didn't do any better. But because I had started moving faster the bastard behind me who was in an inordinate hurry gunned his own engine and ploughed into the back of me—and there I was sandwiched between them, the car I hit and the one that hit me, and hell, you've just heard the rest, it didn't turn out so well. It can't have been Bruce, of course.

It can't have been her, either, in here. The lady in Yellow, and Green, and Red. Too much of a coincidence.

But there you have it. I saw them both. I'll swear on a stack of Bibles.

I mentioned her, my mystery lady, to my analyst at my next session, and of course immediately regretted it, but there it was, out and loose. He had a field day with it, of course. As I knew he would.

"And does she look like anybody you know?"

"If she did I would have said so," I said, sorry I'd brought it up at all. "She's like nobody I've ever seen before—I can't even remember her well enough to describe her right now."

"But you always recognize her."

"Of course I do. She's a dream…" I bit down on the rest of that sentence, but of course it was too late to catch the cat as I let it out of the bag. Dr. Winter, the analyst, leaned back in his chair and steepled his fingers in that pastiche gesture mimicking Freud that really annoyed me—he thought it made him look erudite and oh-so-knowing; it merely made him look like a pretentious clown.

"Ah," he said, sounding as though he had just uncovered the mother lode. "She is your dream?"

"No, she is not," I said, exasperated.

"You've never dreamed about her?"

"I don't even remember her, in between times."

"In between what times?"

"When I see her. Wearing these… colours."

"Colours."

Oh, *damn*. I was throwing him crumbs like there was no tomorrow. I was going to be trussed and tied up and delivered to the Monster of the Id deep in my mind's labyrinth and he would convince me eventually that I was probably acting out, having the Invisible Friend fantasy as a grown man rather than the more usual kid, except that I *was* a grown man and therefore there was this whole deep sexual thing to it that he, Dr. Winter, would help me exorcise from my fevered brain and help me fit into sane society again.

"I have to go," I said abruptly, gathering myself up.

"Oh, but you still have more than fifteen minutes left of the session…" Dr. Winter said, dropping the Freud steeple and reaching out to me with his right hand.

"That's okay," I said.

"You're still paying for the full session," he reminded me.

Figured, of course. But I was no frame of mind to be here. If I had to pay him to be absent, it seemed like a good bargain right then.

"That's fine," I said, taking the few long steps that took me to the door, eager to escape now.

"Next week…?" Dr. Winter said.

"Uh, sure. Yes. Next week."

"She'll wear black, you know."

I was at the door, reaching to open it, and those words made me rear back. "What? What did you say?"

Dr. Winter, who had been leaning forward to make a notation in his file—in *my* file—sat back in his chair and frowned at me. "I said nothing," he stated with the gravitas of a judge.

"You said…"

But it wasn't worth getting into. It would take too long—to explain, to listen.

She'll wear black.

Twice more I saw her. Once she was wearing a hot Fuchsia coat in the middle of a cold gray November day, dawdling along a dripping sidewalk as though she was walking in sunshine when everyone else was monochrome and hurrying to get out of the rain. And once I saw her in a photograph, with a couple of other women wearing nondescript beiges and pale café-au-lait browns. She, of course, was in Blue. Peacock Blue. Glowing.

Looking straight at me out of that photograph.

It was in a newspaper, someplace. I actually cut it out—it didn't have names below, in the caption, which was unusual, but I figured I could at least use the picture to try and find out more—but need I tell you that I lost that thing immediately, and even though I went through the archives of that newspaper later I could never find it again? Flash of colour, gone, par for the course.

I was starting to wonder if Bruce had played a posthumous practical joke on me.

When I could remember enough to think about her at all.

Which I did fairly regularly, actually, every time a flash of vivid colour that might seem oddly out of place caught my eye. But only then. And only for a short moment. And then it was all gone again.

I was forty six years old when they diagnosed the thing that would kill me. And I knew it would kill me. The nurse who took my blood for the tests wore hot pink scrubs but she was not my Lady, and in the days that were left to me I never did see her again.

But I'm in the hospital now, and they tell me that I will never leave this bed again. And yesterday, it was, I think, I caught a glimpse of somebody that might have been her, out in the corridor.

Might have been, except that she wore Black. Deep Black.

And this time she caught my eye and held it, and was not smiling… quite. Except that there was a hint of it below the serious expression she wore on her face. It was as if there was a light beyond a darkness, struggling to come out. It was as though there was something bright, something *yellow*, just underneath those black weeds.

And then she… beckoned.

Well, maybe not. When I looked closer I certainly could not swear to what I thought I'd seen. But I figure… maybe… by tomorrow, or within a day or two, I'll probably have it all figured out.

Maybe Bruce can tell me. He always did know everything. And it was *his* funeral that she came to first, after all.

THE WORD BEHIND THE STORY

Won (Korean): the reluctance on a person's part to let go of an illusion.

THE STORY BEHIND THE WORD

"Won" is another of those English-sounding words that you think you know, that you "recognize" immediately and that will lead you off in a perfectly solid and comfortable but nonetheless completely wrong direction. The other meaning, the one in the Korean context, is something that absolutely NEEDS a word to define it. And this particular story—the vision of the mystery woman, and what she actually means—turns out (although it was written before I learned of this particular word and concept) to beautifully illustrate the idea behind Won.

KINTSUGI

SOMETHING THAT WOULD SHINE

In a city surrounded by high dun-colored walls, on a dun-colored street, in a dun-colored house, behind windows that were no more than high slits through which one could glimpse a dun-colored sky, Jem Marek Agassi wondered again and again what had possessed him to volunteer for this particular position.

Sure, it carried the cachet of the title that went with it—Ambassador to the Mallaseth—but it should have given him pause when he learned that he had been one of only two possible candidates who had stepped forward to be considered for the *voluntary* assignment, and the other guy had, post-application, been locked away for 'observation' after he had attacked, apparently without provocation, an officer on the station where he had been posted.

It should have given him pause for another reason—this could be, almost certainly would be, a one-way trip. There was, to be sure, a remote possibility that he could come home very rich, if very old; but there was a much higher likelihood that he would not return home at all. That all the potential riches and prestige would be wasted on a solitary existence on an alien world at the edge of the galaxy, where his only role would be to ensure the steady supply back to the homeworld of the precious pale crystal spheres which the original negotiators had been informed were commonplace on this world, spilled over the high mountainsides in tumbled profusion. They were considered a nuisance by the Mallaseth, useless except as toys and decoration. Because it would only drive the price up if the true value of the commodity was known to the seller, the humans who had taken part in the original talks had made absolutely certain to agree with that assessment, nodding their heads vigorously when the spheres had been discussed in that disparaging manner, prattling brightly about how delighted their people would be with the new trinkets.

Perhaps it was because of those attitudes that Jem's hosts had generously supplied his Ambassadorial quarters with the things—there was an eye-watering number of them just lying scattered around, apparently without thought or plan, and Jem sometimes felt as though he could weep at the thought of how much wealth had been put within his reach while at the same time making certain that he could make absolutely no use of it whatsoever. Few enough were without some kind of flaw. There were the perfect ones, the kind that Jem had been sent here to collect and obtain, but the majority of them, although always smooth on the outside surface, carried inner damage—cracks that went from one side of the sphere to the other and looked as though they threatened to split it apart on that seam if one but breathed on it too hard, or tiny spider-veined webs deep inside the orbs, barely visible other than in the way they broke and splintered the light, or complex patterns of things that looked almost complicated enough to be hieroglyphics, black or gray or gold or a deep marbled violet against the clear crystal. No two the same. There were times that the cracked and flawed ones seemed far more interesting to Jem, potentially of far more value, at least purely esthetically speaking, than the ones which seemed bland by comparison by having no distinguishing marks in them at all.

But a handful of them—of the perfect and flawless ones— had made their way back to Jem's own homeworld, after the first contacts with offworld civilizations had been tentatively established, and the scientists back home had found an extraordinary use for the crystals. As the heart of a new star drive which would open up the universe for Jem's young and presumptuous race, the crystals were about to become hot property, galaxy-wide—and it had been Jem's primary task, as Ambassador, to ensure that humans got assured, exclusive if possible, and primarily, while their value was still a cypher to the other races, cheap access to the crystals—at least for as long as that was possible.

Jem had no doubt that this place would eventually be humming with trade representatives, trying to get their best bargains out of the stolid, dour local race. It had been his unenviable job to tread the fine line between disparaging these trinkets which held little value to these creatures and offering as little as possible in order to acquire vast quantities of them, and ensuring as far as that was possible that he was the only one who had unfettered access to them.

Like the exploitative colonials of his own people's history, Jem was offering up a handful of beads for the isle of Manhattan. He had less need of diplomacy than of base guile, a golden tongue, and a knack for ingratiation. He had had those gifts in abundance, together with enough cynicism to know that they had been required and the willingness to provide them, while ignoring the still small voice of the conscience that still whispered somewhere in the back of his mind.

The Mallaseth did not help, really. Jem kept a video log of his time here, which included his observations on the milieu in which he found himself. There was a certain value in this, for the anthropologists to pore over in their time, perhaps, but for Jem it was just as important to hear himself talk, to hear a familiar human voice, to keep a grip on who he himself was.

His was a subjective and often snide record. It was just as well that it could not, probably, be fully heard and understood by the Mallaseth, the dominant species of this world. His descriptive entry on them, in the compendium of local lore and knowledge that he was compiling, was less than completely complimentary.

"They call themselves the Mallaseth," he dictated into his computer, in the privacy of his quarters, rather less Ambassadorial (except for the profusion of the crystal spheres) than he had been led to expect might be his, "which, in their language means—of course it does, such words *always* do—The People. They're less than pretty to look at, really. Vaguely humanoid, bipedal, a head which flows more or less directly and necklessly into the torso. With those sloped foreheads, the bugged-out eyes, that thin lipless mouth which runs pretty much across the entire width of their faces like a horizontal gash— all of that makes them look rather like large and somewhat bewildered frogs who don't quite know what to make of the fact that they are walking about upright on their hind legs. They speak amongst themselves in a language I barely recognize as one, and it's something that I can't possibly reproduce. But they're not as stupid as they look to me. The frog-faces conceal hidden talents and a number of them have found it rather less difficult to learn enough of *my* language to be able to carry on a perfectly adequate if not an interesting conversation. Their accents are terrible, but they manage. At this point we simply need to be able to communicate in terms of barter and trade, and that's doable. Just. It helps that they're just a touch telepathic, I think, and sometimes it seems to be enough for them just to have an added dimension of an image of an unfamiliar concept which they seem to just grab from the surface of my thoughts as I try to speak to them. Not entirely sure how I feel about that, really—or just how *much* they are able to get out of my head that way. I wonder if the image of frogs that I always seem to carry about where they're concerned means anything to them, or if they're insulted by it. But, whatever—it doesn't seem to matter—they understand me just fine. And I understand them well enough."

There was more on the Mallaseth—their habits, their manners, their laws. But there was rather less on a somewhat unsettling subject of which Jem had had no warning when he had been dispatched here.

There was another race that lived on the world, out in the mountains where the crystals were.

Arguably they were the true owners of the raw resource Jem had come here to obtain—but they built no cities, living wild off the land, shy and almost invisible; they had no written language at all, it seemed, and the Mallaseth—once Jem had learned of the second race and inquired about them of his hosts—considered them barely sentient savages. They were an embarrassment before the Ambassador, treated as a dirty little secret which the Mallaseth might have preferred to have kept hidden. Jem might have hardly known of their very existence had a handful of them (captives of the Mallaseth, perhaps, or tamed pets, Jem had never been able to pin it down precisely) not been present in the city, and thus inadvertently revealed to his eyes. These others were smaller than the Mallaseth, quicker, more lizard-like than frog-like, and Jem held a private opinion that the Mallaseth had been rather hastily arrogant in their dismissal of this mountain tribe because Jem—from the point of view of the ignorant alien outsider, to be sure, but still— could see a mercurial quick-witted intelligence behind their slit-pupilled eyes, more than he had ever been able to capture, in fact, when looking into the stolid Mallaseth faces.

They rated several entries of their own in his video record.

"The Mallaseth call them the mountain folk. They must have their own name for themselves, of course—and if I asked it might just turn out that it means 'The People'—the word was even less pronounceable and meaningful than the 'Mallaseth'—but it's the frogs who gave me that name for them, not the others themselves," Jem reported into his video journal, frowning thoughtfully as the idea developed in his mind. "I'm less than certain if it's in fact the name they had chosen or if it's a somewhat derogatory term for them by the Mallaseth themselves. Something like we did back in the days of lumping all the Native American tribes as 'redskins'. I don't have the first clue about how to go finding this out for certain, though. Communication with the Mallaseth is rudimentary enough; I have been able to establish no direct communication with the other race at all, at least with the specimens here in the city."

Jem's own subconscious, searching for a suitable mental shorthand he could use for them, had presented him with the concept of Mountiguanas. Direct communication or not, it was obvious in context that the Mountiguanas were held in contempt, and that nobody had even thought to ask them about the crystals which after all came from their country, their mountains. It was the Mallaseth who had made contact with the humans, it was the Mallaseth who had taken it upon themselves to bargain for the thing that the humans wanted, it was the Mallaseth who ran things with a hand so limp-wristed that it might be termed almost tentacle-like but which could still be described as 'iron'. They seemed to be too literal, too stolid, almost too *stupid* (this in the subjective, and undoubtedly deeply ignorant, perspective of the alien who had been appointed Ambassador to their world, and Jem was aware of how judgmental he was being) to be in charge. But they were, in precisely the manner in which an established and top-heavy bureaucracy might have been back home on Earth. Jem had an easy familiarity with this kind of thing. He knew how to deal with it. There were times, in fact, that he was astonished at the ease of communication between himself and the aliens with whom he had been sent to seal this bargain—so long as he assumed them to be cogs in a larger wheel and simply dealt with the wheel itself. Things shook out predictably, in that context.

But the second race, the Mountiguanas, did not really fit into this easy and convenient paradigm, and while Jem was pragmatic enough to dismiss them, in context, as few and irrelevant, that did not prevent him from dwelling on them, on their existence, on their own take on the business relationship which had been built between the humans and the Mallaseth over their heads.

He didn't know just how deeply the Mountiguanas had burrowed into his thoughts until he suddenly conceived an itch to go and actually visit the places from where the Mallaseth gathered the crystals which—when a sufficient quantity of the suitably flawless specimens had been put together—would be placed on the ship which had brought Jem here, and which would be given the coordinates of Earth and then (as a redundancy) would be met when it approached the home system, and escorted the rest of the way home. All of this had been done the slow way—Jem had arrived here on what had essentially been built to be that cargo ship, in a jury-rigged cryosleep passenger compartment in which he had almost exclusively slept through the *years* it had taken to get him here; it would take those same *years* for the ship to return, bearing its crystal treasure, but then, if everything worked out according to the way the scientists thought, the next ship that turned up at the Mallaseth planet would arrive in a considerably shorter time. It was only then that everything would begin to pay off for Jem. If he was still alive; if he was still in good enough physical shape to actually enjoy any of it at all. He was fully aware of the risks he had signed on for when he had accepted this assignment—the risks, and the responsibilities. So far, he had been coming through on the responsibility front, doing the things he had been sent here to do without thinking too hard about the moral ramifications of the entire enterprise. But there had been nothing about the Mountiguanas in the scant materials he had studied before he arrived here—and he had not been able to bring himself to simply disregard them as irrelevant once he had become aware of their existence.

The Mallaseth had simply offered up the crystals in exchange for things they deemed to be of more value, for them. The stuff was known to come from the mountains, it was known to be plentiful there (or so the humans had been told) but before Jem no human had set foot on this world at all, and not even Jem had seen the actual physical sites from where the Mallaseth obtained the crystals (So valuable! So easily and artlessly dismissed as valueless trinkets when that was suitable!). It had been kind of taken for granted that these were not the places where he would wish to go, or be encouraged to visit.

And it seemed as though this was the point where communications conveniently broke down with his hosts, because there seemed to be no way Jem could get through to his usual Mallaseth contacts that he wanted a guide to the mountains where the crystals originated. He was stonewalled with what he quickly became convinced was deliberately cultivated incomprehension. It was as though he had suddenly committed a serious social faux-pas, and his hosts were trying to shield him from the potential fallout by simply ignoring the fact that anything untoward had happened at all.

His suspicions that the Mountiguanas had more native intelligence than anyone was letting on was confirmed when, on his way back to his quarters from a less-than-usually productive meeting with one of his Mallaseth handlers, he strode along an empty corridor lit in that weird non-localized light the Mallaseth seemed to have perfected for the insides of buildings which seemed designed to let in as little outside light as they could. He was frustrated and annoyed, in the grip of a kind of bleak questioning mood, wondering if the choice to come here had been one of the worst decisions of his life after all, when he became aware of a tendril of thought which was utterly and completely unlike any of that. A light, questioning, interrogative touch, very gentle, almost a diffident knock on the closed door of his mind.

If he had stopped to think about it, he might never have been able to accomplish what he did next at all—but in just the right kind of mindset, without pausing to give too much consideration to anything... he *opened the door.*

And then froze, when he became aware that he was no longer alone inside his own head.

::*we are sorry*::

"What?" he said, out loud.

::*we are sorry we know we intrude we know this may not be best way we are sorry maybe better if get out of public place where observed home maybe and we hear even without loud*::

Startled, Jem raked the corridor with his eyes but could see nothing extraordinary, nothing that would present him with this bewildering communication. And yet he knew, knew beyond a shadow of a doubt, what that something must be. And the idea that he was communicating—and communicating in this direct manner, after so long a period of patient plodding pedestrian attempts at exchanging information with the Mallaseth—with the race that the Mallaseth deemed to be so far beneath themselves, was enough to make his mind start turning somersaults.

Jem took the invisible presence at its word, and hurried forward again, now eager to gain the privacy of his quarters. He did so without further incident or further communication (although he could still sense, disconcertingly, the tiny tendril, the presence, of that *other* inside his own skull) and it was only after the door to the outside was securely closed and he stood leaning against it facing into the solitude of his sitting room that the alien intelligence spoke to him again.

::*we understand why you are here we mourn we have lost so much already we keep losing so much because the others do not care do not understand but we know you want to see we know they do not want you to go we know they do not want you to understand*::

"Understand what?" Jem said, quietly. He had a sense that speaking out loud was not required, that his thoughts would be conveyed just as he was 'hearing' the other's—but somehow he could not bring himself to do that, not now, not yet. To him communication was speech. He felt the other contemplate the warning that speech was unnecessary, even dangerous—and then come to an understanding of his point of view—and accept it, and simply send a wordless warning of 'quiet, quiet, they must not hear, they must not know'.

::*we want you to see we want your others to see we want to show truth we can show you mountains*::

"You want to take me…? To your home?"

::*yes home we want to take home show you truth you do not know you do not understand they know they understand they do not want you to know*::

Jem knew that an unsanctioned expedition like this would probably make his situation here untenable—he was basically dependent wholly on the goodwill and the support of the Mallaseth and if he offended them it might go hard on him— from both the Mallaseth and, if they chose to expel him for breaking some taboo or another, from his own people whose plans his actions might have set back years, if not scuttled permanently. There was certainly no way that he could conceal such an expedition from the Mallaseth—he was the only human on the planet, after all, and his absence would be immediately and painfully obvious. And there were other concerns—this was, after all, an alien world. One whose gravity and whose air were good enough that Jem could exist here without any major external support—but the Mallaseth did supplement the oxygen content of the air inside his own quarters, which did make it easier to breathe. On the few occasions that he had ventured outside into the streets of the Mallaseth city Jem had definitely felt the difference, the absence of that oxygen—not enough to injure him or render him incapacitated but any kind of strenuous exercise would have been completely out of the question, and the mountains were not exactly close to the city. This would be a trek fraught with both physical and social peril. He had so much to lose—so much—everything, in fact—and yet he already knew that he would go.

And so did the thing in his mind.

::we will make arrangements we will let you know be ready::

"All right," Jem said softly, his mouth curving into an odd little smile. "I will be ready."

They informed him later that evening, in the same disconcerting manner, where he could find a carefully concealed Mallaseth scooter and then simply put it into his mind directly how to operate it; the city was a walled one (although Jem had never been able to establish a reason for this) and the gates, which did stand open during the daylight hours thus throwing the purpose of the city walls into even deeper mystery and confusion, *were* closed, even if only symbolically, at sundown. But not locked. It was easy enough, just before dawn of the next day, to sneak the purloined scooter through dark and empty streets, and nobody showed up to protest when Jem pulled one of the massive gates open just wide enough to let him and the scooter out. There was no apparent way to close the gate from the outside, though, and he all but resigned himself to his defection becoming known sooner rather than later—he was leaving rather an obvious trail. But the voice inside his head assured him that his new friends would take care of that particular detail, and then directed him away from the city walls, towards the mountains which loomed blue and purple on the horizon brightening with the imminent advent of the blood-orange sun.

Distances were deceptive in this alien world, and the mountains proved to be a lot closer than they looked—Jem reached them in only a few hours of hard riding across the packed dun-colored plain (this held no surprise for him. This was a colorless world, and the Mallaseth appeared to utterly lack the motherwit to miss the presence of color—they themselves were largely the same nondescript shade as the rest of their world and that seemed to satisfy their needs perfectly). But the mountains themselves… were not dun-colored. When Jem approached them, he became aware of vegetation which gave them a tinge of red and gold, like fall foliage in the temperate parts of Earth where such seasons held sway. And the ground underneath held rich dark soil, and pale grey stone.

The terrain climbed, first gently and then, abruptly, rising up into vertical bluffs of pearly grey rock. The ground underneath the scooter's wheels finally became too steep and too rough for the conveyance and Jem was instructed to abandon it in a shallow cave underneath one of the buttresses and continue on foot. It was slow going because he had to stop so often to rest and catch his breath, gasping for air like a trout out of water, and his hosts (it was inevitable to think of them as that, he had been *invited*) waited patiently for him to recover and then urged him on, forward, up.

Until he finally turned a corner and came upon that which he had come here to see.

In a deep cleft in the rocks, a soft pulsing light drew Jem's attention and then commanded his approach.

::*do not be surprised do not be upset do not be bewildered*::

The voice inside his head was almost pleading, and Jem frowned, wondering what it was that he should be steeling himself to see. But the very first thing he did notice was that the floor of the cavern into which he now stepped was awash with the crystal orbs he had come to this world to secure. They had always seemed so fragile but it seemed to be okay to walk upon them, and Jem did, with care, because he was urged onward, deeper. The light changed as he penetrated further and then all of sudden he became aware that there were different intensities of light all around him and the reason behind that was simply that parts of the glowing crystalline walls of the cave were obscured by shadowy shapes which were outlined in silhouette against them. Mountiguanas. Facing those walls. With their hands laid against the crystal, reverently, gently. Humming something low and—well—and *holy*…

Jem watched in both horror and fascination as one of the entities by the wall appeared to come to an end of its song; it folded its hands, and a part of the wall seemed to come away cradled between them.

A crystal sphere.

The entity holding it stood there for a moment staring at the thing in its hands, and then laid it down very gently at its feet against the wall of crystal from which it had been taken and shuffled away with its head bowed and its eyes downcast, the empty hands still folded together before him as though in an echo of a prayer.

Jem squinted at the crystal ball which had just been abandoned, afraid to approach.

::no go look it is why you came take a look do you understand::

The new ball rested against the crystal wall, still looking soft and not yet completely formed, pulsing faintly. It was not one of the valuable pristine ones, this one had a dark branched crack deep inside which seemed—

::no no you still do not understand it is not the clear ones which are of value::

"They are, to us," Jem murmured, reaching out to the new ball.

::do not touch yet it is not yet whole it is not yet complete but look at the others the hard ones you can pick those up you can touch them what do you see::

"You're right, I don't understand," Jem said, but felt as though he was failing them somehow by not doing so. He picked up one of the spheres, a second, a third; he stared into them. They each had their own character. Their own story.

Their own story…

They had no written language. So Jem had been repeatedly told. And yet the images that persistently lingered in his mind when he looked at these spheres—clumsy ones, and by this Jem knew that they had not been his own idea, had been an attempt to explain and had been introduced by the creatures who had brought him here—were books. Vast volumes, books which (if he had been asked to describe in image alone what the concept meant to him) represented… ancient histories. Old, old books, Gilt-edged. Leather-bound. Pages fragile with the passage of countless years.

A legacy. A history. A mythology. The treasures of an

entire people… brought here, and delivered, mind by mind, caught and frozen into moments, into these spheres, trapped by precious and precise flaws in the stone…

They had no written language. Of course they did not. They had no need of one.

Their stories… their stories…

::*you understand*::

The tone was one of muted triumph.

Jem stared at the spheres in his hand with horrified pity. "Not yet. But I am beginning to. They're stealing your past, aren't they? The Mallaseth? And then… then they told *us* that this was for sale… and it was never theirs, never theirs to sell…"

::*so many lines broken so many stories unfinished so many stories with holes we can not ever fill so much lost so much*::

"But the perfect ones…? The ones without flaw?"

::*they have no value they have no story they belong to children who have not lived enough yet to have something to tell or sometimes the final farewell of someone who no longer has the strength to pass on the story they are no longer part of the story it is the others that tell the story*::

"How do we understand the story?" gasped Jem. "How do we ever understand this?"

::*we come here end of every year after we mature we come we tell the stones we put our memory into the spheres then leave behind this place has many spheres many years many memories but they have taken the record is broken the memory is lost so much lost we can never get back never get back never get back*::

"The Mallaseth… do they know? Do they really understand?"

::*they understand they have their own ways they do not care what is lost*::

"But it is to you that we should make payment, not to them—if this is a thing that can even be *sold*—they have done nothing but steal, and enslave…"

::*we cannot sell no price but the ones you call perfect the ones that do not carry a story that do not carry a part of one of us you may take for no payment because they are valueless but do not take the ones with*::

story inside we lose we lose we lose::

There was going to be hell to pay back home, when this became known. If Jem lived to make it known. He was suddenly very afraid to go back to the Mallaseth city, under their influence, under their control. They had shown that they could supplement his oxygen, in order to make him more comfortable. They could just as easily adjust his air... in more lethal ways. Get a new Ambassador sent when they regretfully reported Jem's death. Someone else. Someone different. Someone new. Someone to whom they would never make the mistake of showing the others at all. Not only would the history and the legacy of the Mountiguanas be threatened—their very existence might be, if the ruthless Mallaseth took steps to remove them, to stop them from scuttling a commercial deal they found valuable.

"They couldn't," Jem muttered. "They *wouldn't*. Not genocide. Besides, they would need some—to keep coming here—to keep making these..."

But the images that were put into his head at that thought made him cry out and drop the spheres in his hands, covering his eyes. Images of these gentle creatures in chains before these holy walls, making the things that the Mallaseth would sell. And more and more of them would turn out as those pristine perfect sterile ones that the Mallaseth would particularly prize, as more and more of their makers stopped thinking, feeling, remembering, finding the cracks in the crystal and filling them with their past, their imperfect past, sealing the imperfections in the stone with a record of their own flawed lives and making every sphere irreplaceable, unique... until all were dead, all the minds were dead, and the only thing that remained was a dead-eyed, mind-stilled creature whose instinct was to carve out the perfect crystal balls but with no memory of what they really ought to have been. An army of slave-ants, made mindless and compliant, churning out a thing on which their masters would grow rich and prosperous.

::you must you must you must....::

It was a hard road ahead, but Jem could see no other. There would be no riches, no long life of quiet opulence, no retirement—probably even censure and disgrace, in place of that, if they decided to go that far, in his absence.

He could not return to the Mallaseth, whom he no longer trusted. But he could not go home.

He had to gather up what empty soulless spheres he could carry, retrieve the shuttle which had brought him down to the surface, and return to his ship, in orbit above the sullen dun-colored world. He had to set the ship on a return course, just as had been planned—but its payload would not be just the treasure it had come here to carry, it would also hold a full record of the truth behind the spheres so essential to mankind's leap into the stars... and then Jem would send it all home. With a clear message. The Mallaseth must be bypassed, ignored—there must be a warning posted against them to anyone who came near—if the spheres were to be had at all it would be at the hands of the mountain people, who had already said they would ask no price for them so long as the others, the ones they truly valued, were protected and preserved.

The Mallaseth would not take this development meekly. Jem had learned enough of them to know that much. They were petty and vindictive and small-minded, greedy and ruthless, and they would do what they felt they needed to do in order to claim what they felt was their due. The mountain folk would stand, as best they could. As for Jem…

There was no real provision of himself returning on that ship, anyway—and it was just as well, then, that he himself would then take the shuttle back down, probably crash-land it in some mountain clearing, and prepare to defend the mountain fastness as best he was able against the potential backlash from the denizens of the dun-colored city.

And someday—maybe someday when his own people might learn to read and interpret the histories written in the flaws in the spheres of memory—someone might read of his own end there.

All Jem could do was hope that the story of his life would find a magnificent crack, and fill it with something that would shine.

THE WORD BEHIND THE STORY

Kintsugi (Japanese): "golden repair", the Japanese art of fixing broken pottery with lacquer resin dusted or mixed with powdered gold, silver, or platinum (the "golden repair"). As a philosophy it speaks to breakage and repair becoming part of the history of an object, rather than something to disguise.

THE STORY BEHIND THE WORD

What if the thing that looked broken, looked damaged, the thing that we might instinctively disregard, turns out to be the most valuable thing of all? What if our criteria for value were utterly different from somebody else's—what if their treasures were considered, by us, to be garbage, or vice versa? What is it that gives us the right to think that our own idea of what is "perfect" is the only one that is valid, or valuable? And what if things that were "damaged" by the simple fact that they hold memory or history—that our past itself has "damaged" them, to the point that they are witness to it—were valued precisely because they held this treasure, this information, this trust, and without the cracks or crevices or broken sharp edges these things would be nothing more than valueless, smooth, featureless, commonplace cheap baubles whose existence is yet to unfold, whose truths are yet to be told, and until that happens they are merely a blank canvas on which it is possible to preserve a lesson, a dream, or an idea?

YA'ABURNEE

THE FLYING DUTCHMAN

The smoke never cleared in Chandler's Bar. The man who used to be known there as Mikey O'Halloran could remember the place vividly from twenty years ago. It appeared not to have changed at all—the same fading, dog-eared posters hung off the gray-green walls, the same initials were carved into the trestles, it might even have been the same bartender behind the bar. The men who used to drink here with Mikey were gone, of course, but their places had been taken by a copycat generation which wore the same dingy T-shirts revealing the same tattoos on the same muscled biceps that Mikey O'Halloran's mates once rippled under the yellow light in Chandler's. And the same smoke, pearly, pungent, eternal, hung in the air like incense in some pagan temple.

Mikey O'Halloran alone had changed. Changed a lot. Enough to be uneasy in Chandler's where once he knew and was known by everybody and everything. Mikey O'Halloran was now Michael Halloran, the name that went with the Pulitzer they'd given him the previous year. He had worked hard to shed the rough, working Irish in him. He had succeeded. And he was damned if he knew what absurd instinct made him return to this hellhole. So many years had passed; surely too many...

He rubbed his cheek with the back of his hand, and stepped up to the bar.

"Whiskey," he said by way of reply to the taciturn barman's inquiring eyebrow. "Make it a double."

The smoke thinned for a moment, making way for a fresh wave, and Michael's eyes, slipping back into a habit he'd thought lost, used the respite to rake the faces that hung over the long tables. There had been a momentary lull when he had walked in, out of place in his posh-sailor's clothes which had all too obviously never felt salt spray; but once the incumbent customers had given him the long, measured stare they accorded all novelties, the trawlermen and riggers and stevedores had gone back to their own conversations and flatly ignored him. He was too far removed from this place to recognize any of the trestled faces—he was even a little afraid, now that he was here and knowing these men as well as he did. But then, just as the smoke thickened again, Michael forgot the momentary stab of fear and straightened sharply as though somebody had rammed a red-hot poker through his spine.

There. In the corner. The old man in the knitted cap.

But it couldn't possibly be, for all that he had come here hoping to find him. The old man of twenty years ago had been old even then, and surely by this time... No, it was impossible. But Michael took a few hesitant steps in the old man's direction all the same, nursing his drink between his palms.

The old man, his hair coming out in tufted wisps from beneath a shapeless knitted cap that used to be red but was now a faded, dusty pink, sat hunched over his own glass. Beside him, on the sticky table marked by generations of rings left behind by other glasses, rested a plain pipe, which was quite out. He could have been one of any number of old sea dogs but Michael sucked in his breath as his eyes fell on the old man's hands. The little finger on the left hand was completely missing, the ring finger stumped at the first joint. Michael had been there when those wounds had been sustained. There could be no doubt. None at all.

"Van Doorn," he said, very softly.

In the background buzz of loud conversation, raucous laughter and unidentified noises coming from behind the bar, the old man looked up at the sound of his name. He squinted at Michael's face through the yellow-lit smoke for a moment, and then his mouth tugged upwards into an economical little smile, no wider than it had to be.

"Well," he said, "so it's you." He spoke in a flat, accented

English, his words slow, as though he were choosing each with care. He gestured with the mutilated hand. "Sit."

"You're still here?" said Michael, slipping into the indicated seat. "When I left, you were going off to South America."

"I was there," said Van Doorn. "I am back."

"Are you still on that virago of a ship of yours?"

"Ja. She and I are still together. You, it seems, have been a long time from the sea."

"You can tell," said Michael, and it was half question, half sarcastic remark.

"Oh, ja," said Van Doorn seriously. "A drop on those fine breeches of yours, and they would be done for. No, you have been off ship for a long time. You walk like one who is used to dry land."

"I am a writer now," said Michael, and it sounded defensive, with the hollow, ringing air of a vintage lame excuse.

But Van Doorn nodded sagely. "Ja? What is it that you write?"

"I wrote... about you," said Michael. "You and the *Juliana*. The two of you... I have never forgotten."

"And people read this, what you have written?"

"Yes. They even gave me a prize for it. The Pulitzer."

"Ah. The Pulitzer." Van Doorn sounded as though he knew all about the award, but dismissed it as of no consequence to himself. Which was probably the literal truth, or at least the second half of it was. "But what is there to write? I fish, I and *Juliana* fish, then I sell the fish, and the money goes home. To Gerda, and the children."

Now Michael knew why he had returned, looking for this old man, hoping to find him here against all odds. It was to tell him something. And while Michael Halloran had doubted that he would ever see the old man again, Mikey O'Halloran, one-time deck hand on the trawler *Juliana*, had known that the old captain would be there.

"Van Doorn," Michael said, "I've met Gerda."

For the first time the old man's eyes betrayed him. He first looked startled, then the expression metamorphosed into a deep and abiding sorrow, graven into his seasoned face. If nobody ever noticed it there it was only because Van Doorn kept it at bay by keeping his features schooled, his eyes slitted against the glare of sun on sea and shuttered on the pain within. "Ja?" he said at length, very softly. "It has been... a long time."

Michael's throat closed. There was no way he could tell this man about the day that Gerda had come to see him. The bitter and angry woman who had recognized her life in his novel and had come to do... she knew not what; the woman who had ended up weeping in his living room for over two hours as she had poured out her real story to him, filling in the blanks he had omitted when he had told it to the world. The story of a child-bride who bore five children in seven years, and then watched her husband wave goodbye from a clapped-out old trawler once named *Sparrowhawk* and re-christened *Juliana,* after his eldest daughter—watched him go sailing off into the endless blue horizon in order to feed them all, because there was no work. The money he sent came sporadically, but he never came home again—he had sworn not to return until he could do so as a prosperous man. But prosperity eluded him. He and *Juliana* were always one step ahead of disaster.

Van Doorn had been ten years away from home when the young Mikey O'Halloran had joined him on the trawler. They had been five years together after that. In that time Mikey learned of the wife, the children; understood the name of Van Doorn's ship to have been born of an unceasing longing for the child that had been less than eight years old at the time her father had left, the child that Van Doorn had tried to keep in his life by giving his ship her name.

"For years I waited, hoped," Gerda had said to Michael back in his apartment. "I kept on telling the children, someday. I tried to believe that myself. But hopes die. Mine did. The children grew. He still sent money, but it was not enough, it was never enough..."

She took on odd jobs, to keep her children fed and clothed. She had held out heroically, but she was no more than human after all, a lonely woman who had never bargained for spending her life alone. It became clear to her after the many years with no word except the crumpled dollars from various parts of the world that Van Doorn wasn't coming back. So Gerda buried him. Somewhere in the United States stood the gravestone of a man still living and plying the oceans, a man who did not know, never would, that he was a ghost.

"I remarried," Gerda had confessed, almost guiltily, as though she had murdered Van Doorn with her own hands. "I have been married now for ten years. He is a lovely man, and treats me well. And my children. Here, these are pictures... that's Jan and his wife, and his two little boys... and there, that's Juliana, on her wedding day... and this, this is Meredith Maude. That's Juliana's little daughter. She will be nine in December." She had pressed the snapshots into Michael's hands, her need palpable but unarticulated. "Do you think he is still alive?"

"I don't know," Michael had said. "I honestly do not know."

She had closed his hands around the pictures. "Keep them," she said. "And if you ever run across him again..."

He pulled the photographs out of his pocket now and pushed them across the table at Van Doorn.

"Here," he said, "Gerda wanted you to have these."

Van Doorn peered at the pictures myopically, obscured as they were by the tangible atmosphere of Chandler's bar. His hands trembled as he picked up the photo of little dark-haired Meredith Maude, his never-seen granddaughter. He glanced up at Michael over the edge of the photo, smiling.

"That is Juliana," he said. "That is my child."

"No," said Michael.

Van Doorn had slid the picture aside, and now sat staring at the photo of a slender young girl in white, smiling dreamily at the camera.

"Who is this?" asked the old man. His voice told Michael that he already knew the answer to that question, and was only asking it because he was desperately hoping that Michael was going to tell him he was wrong.

"Juliana," said Michael gently. "That is Juliana. The little girl... her name is Meredith, and she is Juliana's child."

Van Doorn was already looking at the next picture. "And this is Jan," he said, his gaze stiff and pained on his only son. "Ja?"

"Yes," said Michael. "Jan, and Elizabeth, and those two are Hank and Frederic."

"Hank?"

"Short for Henry, I think."

"Hendri. That is my name," said Van Doorn in a hollow voice.

"I know," said Michael.

They sat in silence for a while. Michael knocked back the remains of his double whiskey in one gulp, and shivered. Van Doorn looked somehow shrunken. Useless. All these years he had laboured for a family, and the family had gone on and left him behind.

"What else did she tell you, my Gerda?" he said suddenly, jolting Michael out of a reverie.

"Nothing much," Michael lied. The gravestone was not his secret.

"Are they happy?" Van Doorn asked, with a strange pathos. "Tell me that. Are they happy?"

"Yes," said Michael. It was true, as far as he knew. "And all the grandchildren get told stories about their famous sea captain grandfather. None of them have been allowed to grow up in ignorance of you."

What was it that Gerda had called those stories? The tales of the Flying Dutchman? That, too, was something that Van Doorn would never learn from his lips.

"That's what he is, isn't it?" Gerda had asked, a little bitterly. "That is all he has ever been. Their father. My husband. All that counted for nothing. It was to be a legend to them that he left them. He could not bear the thought of being an ordinary man in his children's eyes."

"Will you be seeing her again? Gerda?" asked Van Doorn humbly.

"I don't know. No. Probably not."

"Did she ask about me?"

"Yes."

"Did she tell you to tell me anything?"

"Only... that she is sorry. About the way things turned out. She really did love you, you know."

Van Doorn sighed, his fingers caressing the photograph of his granddaughter. He made no reply for a long time to Michael's words. Then, with another deep sigh, he got up and picked up his pipe and then, with some hesitation, the pictures. Michael noticed the slight pause and pushed the photos forward gently.

"Keep them, they're for you."

"Did she ask if I had any message?" Van Doorn asked, photos clutched awkwardly in his maimed hand, the hand that *Juliana* had marked to seal him to her.

"Do you?" asked Michael, sidestepping.

Van Doorn started moving away even as he spoke, and his words appeared to come, appropriately enough, from a spirit wreathed in sulphurous fumes of Hell.

"Tell her," said the old man, "that I am still at the wheel."

THE WORD BEHIND THE STORY

Ya'aburnee (Arabic): Both morbid and beautiful at once, this incantatory word means "You bury me," a declaration of one's hope that they'll die before another person because of how difficult it would be to live without them.

THE STORY BEHIND THE WORD

This one... well, it's an older story. And I kept on looking at it, and wondering if it fits this. And it does... and it doesn't. But every time I thought that it didn't I'd look at it again and there was an aftertaste of it. The great love. The love that means everything. An obsessive love, even. And look at it this way. How if you took this story—really—to be about that ship, the Juliana, binding its master to her with bonds so unbreakable that he would give up everything for her—even a real woman?

DUENDE

THE PAINTING

It always gave Molly a shock to realize how little the museum changed from year to year. Returning here was beginning to feel like going back in time, and simply arriving at the worn front step again and again at the same instant in her life.

This year something was different, though. Through a glass partition she could see into the curator's office as she walked in, and she glanced in as she always did—in the last few years the ancient guardian of this tiny museum had started to recognize her, and had even raised a gnarled hand in greeting. Today the office was tenanted by a much younger man. He looked up with a friendly but blank smile as she walked past. Molly avoided his eyes, shuffled past with her hands in her pockets. She felt irrationally upset. How could they? How could they change things? This was supposed to be immutable, unchanging, the anchor point in a constantly shifting universe. She wondered briefly and morbidly if the bushy-browed old curator was dead.

Her feet took her unbidden to the same painting she always came to see. Molly could almost see the floor worn into a subtle groove along this path, she had walked it so many times before. She kept her eyes down until the last minute, as always, relishing the shock of lifting them to the painting—it was a sort of delicious pain, something that tore into her and released a bittersweet sort of rush, a longing for something never had and a sense of loss of something long had and cherished all rolled into one. But this time she wasn't alone here, as usual. Her eyes, still downcast, met a pair of paint-splattered sneakers, and then travelled upwards along a none-too-clean orange overall to meet the quizzical glance of a young man leaning against the wall.

They stood looking at one another for a moment or two.

"What are you doing?" Molly blurted at last, when the silence stretched into being acutely uncomfortable.

He didn't seem to find the question in the least bit disconcerting.

"It's going into storage," he said easily, tossing his head in the direction of Molly's painting.

"Storage?" she echoed. The word was meaningless. This painting had to hang here, *right* here, or else the world would fly apart and Molly Cameron would no longer know who she was or what ideals she lived her life by.

"Yeah," said the young workman lightly. "Into the back room."

"Why?" Molly asked, and to her chagrin felt tears gather in her eyes. She slid her gaze from the young man's face and on to the painting, but discovered that it was blurred and indistinct through the tears. She had been coming here since she was very young, to worship at this shrine; she knew every delicate detail of the painting, and yet now she could not quite see it clearly, and could not remember it.

"Search me," the young man said after a beat of silence.

He was distantly friendly, willing to wait until she had had her gawk to get on with the job. But get on with it he would, and Molly found herself hating him for it.

"Don't you have anything else to do?" Molly asked, nastily for her, knuckling her eyes.

"Eh?" the other said, sounding genuinely surprised. Then he seemed to take in her damp eyes, the clenched hands, the glance at the painting. "You like this one, don't you? Don't be upset—they kinda change them round every so often, I'm sure it'll be right out again before you know it."

"But not *there*," Molly whispered. "It's been hanging there, just so, for years. For years! Even if they put it back, it'll be somewhere else... It'll be different. It means..."

"What?" he said. He was intrigued; this reaction to what seemed to be a relatively minor incident was wildly too strong.

Molly must have been radiating her distress, because in the next pause, while she fought to gain control of her breath, they were joined by the new curator, who approached wanting to know if there was a problem.

"You can't take it away," Molly said, clutching at his sleeve, at his authority.

He freed his arm with some distaste. "Madam," he said, with a commendable effort at not allowing that distaste to creep into his voice, "we do need to rotate our stock occasionally, it gives the place a facelift—we can't just stay static forever..."

"But it's a museum. Museums preserve..."

"We thought we would use this gallery for an Impressionistic exhibition. We do have in our possession a genuine Manet..."

"But this *is* genuine. It's the only real thing you have..."

The curator stared at the offending painting with a jaundiced eye. "That?" he said. "That, Madam, is a certified fake."

The breath went out of Molly in a long sigh. "Fake?"

"It was originally supposed to be a genuine Luckenberg, but we've had it valued for insurance, and it's a fake."

"Who's Luckenberg?"

The curator stared at her. "Lord Henry Luckenberg? He painted the landscape around here a lot, and an occasional portrait. That's why this painting was thought to be so rare. It's not his usual subject matter. But the lady was thought to have been Matilda, his bride—she drowned after they'd been married for less than a fortnight, in Reedmere. But it's not Luckenberg at all."

"Does that matter?"

"What?"

Molly and the curator stared at each other in blank incomprehension of each other's worlds. It was left to the young workman to bridge the silence. The painting had been just a painting to him, a load—something to be removed from this wall, taken into the storage area, and dumped there. Now he was looking at it and seeing it properly for the first time: a young woman veiled in white, with her eyes glowing blue and joyous behind the gauze, extending a fragile, pale hand towards that person whom she loved with all her being and who waited just outside the frame ready to receive her.

"That's not fake," the young man said abruptly.

Both Molly and the curator turned towards him as one, but he seemed to be oblivious of them. He stretched out a hand so that his fingers almost touched those of the young bride, and for a moment it seemed that her eyes were focused on him alone. "God," he said, "to have someone look at you like that. To know that it's *possible*. That's not fake. That's the realest thing in the world."

"It's a painting," snapped the curator.

"It's a vow," said Molly. The young man turned to her, his own eyes bright, nodding.

"You," said the curator suddenly, pointing at Molly. "I've seen you here before, haven't I?"

"I come every year," Molly said.

"Every year?"

Molly did not want to explain. This was hers, *hers*, and nobody else in the world had the right to know it. Not even the man with the power to take it from her, the petty autocrat glowering at her with his foot beating an impatient tattoo on the polished wooden floor. Especially not him. But then she glanced at the young workman, and something in the eyes of the youth she had come close to hating a moment ago gave her strength.

"Today would have been my wedding anniversary," she said, very softly, so that both men instinctively bent forward to hear. "My... fifty-eighth anniversary, as it happens. I come here every year on what would have been my wedding day... to find out why I couldn't marry Willie."

The curator was bristling again but the young workman was nodding as understanding dawned. He waited, however, for her to take a deep breath and finish her own confession.

"You see," she said, "I could not do that." Her hand lifted briefly, helplessly, towards the painting and then dropped back to her side. "I could not look at him like that. I could not feel that. And if I could not do it on my wedding day... then I could not... I could not...." She wiped at her eyes again. "Today would have been my wedding anniversary," she said again, the words dying into a whisper, settling on the painting like a fine dust.

She looked up at the painting again, as though hypnotised by it. The loving eyes on the canvas were both a blessing on what she had sacrificed—renouncing what might have been less than perfect and holding out for that slice of heaven which the painting-bride promised could exist—and a never-ending reproach which stretched through her lonely years, for letting go of something which was not heaven but which might have given her an imperfect, possibly flawed, but *human* happiness. The painting had been a riddle, and Molly, throughout all the years she had been coming here, was yet to discover whether she had got it right. And now it was going to be taken, even that—years ago she had lost Willie at the command of the loving, lethal lady in white; now she was going to lose the lady herself. There had been no answers—and now, very soon, there would be no question.

Helpless, defeated, the old woman turned unsteadily and walked towards the door. The curator stared after her, his hands limp at his sides, his mouth open. Then he tore his eyes away and looked at the painting again—the hot blue eyes behind the veil, the reaching hand... He suddenly shivered.

"Take it," he said hoarsely. "Take it away and bury it somewhere, deep. Let nobody ever find it again."

"It isn't a fake," murmured the young man again.

The curator turned away, hunched into himself. "That," he said, softly and distinctly, "is why it must go."

The young man bit his lip, turned, lifted the painting down, and laid it gently face down against the wall, blinding the blue eyes behind the veil.

There was a faint shape on the wall, a trace of where the painting had hung untouched for years; the wall looked curiously bare without it, almost indecent.

And the room was suddenly full of shadows, and then it was full of light.

THE WORD BEHIND THE STORY

Duende (Spanish): While originally used to describe a mythical, spritelike entity that possesses humans and creates the feeling of awe of one's surroundings in nature, its meaning has transitioned into referring to "the mysterious power that a work of art has to deeply move a person."

THE STORY BEHIND THE WORD

This story once upon a time won me a BBC Short Story Award. I think that might have been because (once again) it illustrates a concept, an idea—perhaps it is not what immediately comes to mind when this particular Spanish word is uttered, but it fits, it fits beautifully, the particular work of art described in this story moves a person deeply enough to change her life, to channel her entire existence in a direction she never expected or wanted. I don't know that I can come up with a greater or more vivid example of Duende.

SAUDADE

THE BONES OF OUR ANCESTORS, THE BLOOD OF OUR FLOWERS

They passed like shadows in the night, the two of them—the old man with a mattock slung over his shoulder and the boy with an empty sack dangling from one hand. The old man's eyes sometimes caught what little light there spilled from the waning moon in the clear sky above as he glanced around him watching for other moving shadows; the hand resting on the handle of his mattock seemed casual but in fact everything about him was tense, wary, waiting for unseen danger. The boy swung from trudging along dutifully and stifling a yawn every so often to occasionally catching his companion's mood and looking around in the abrupt panic-stricken manner of a startled rabbit.

Nothing else moved in the night except the two of them, but the old man clung to the edge of the trees and what concealment they offered, and did not break out into the open field until he absolutely had to. Even then, he hesitated for the longest time, raking the trees and the meadow for danger before he stepped out into the open.

"Come," he whispered, speaking for the first time. "Hurry. We have little time."

The boy yawned. "Grandfather, why are we…"

"Hush. If you do not understand already, now is not the time. Stay alert."

"What are we looking for?"

The old man paused for a moment, glancing up at the sky. "Once, perhaps, angels," he said abruptly. "Tonight, who knows what demons walk. Follow. Be quiet, and be wary."

They stepped out into the grass, and a cool breeze they had not felt under the trees reached out to caress their cheeks, wrapped stray blades of the long grass around their ankles.

"How do you know where to look?" the boy said, dropping his voice even lower. "There's a whole field…"

We know. We have always known. This is your blood, your heritage, you should be able to walk on this field and find what we've come here to seek without pause, without thinking. I could have—I could have, if only these old bones did not get in the way… this belongs to both of us, boy. This is our past… but this is your future…

The old man's thoughts were harsh… but he had said nothing. Not out loud. And the silence settled on both of them, gently, like the touch of a moth's wings. And out there on the field, in the dimness of the pallid moonlight and the glitter of distant stars, the grasses shimmered and stirred, as if the field were breathing. No, as if it were holding its breath…

The boy swung the empty sack he carried. "Grandfather," he said carefully, "it's *bulbs…*"

The old man's eyes glinted again as he turned briefly to glance at his grandson, and this time the glint was more than just moonlight on a reflective surface. This time it was moonlight on water. The old man's cheeks were streaked with tears, and more brimmed in the corner of his eye. "Some day," he whispered, turning away again. "Some day, you will understand. These are the bones and the blood of our ancestors…"

The boy suddenly flung out a pointing finger, squinting into the half-light. "What's *that?*"

The old man followed the line of the boy's hand, allowed his gaze to linger on what looked like freshly turned earth, bitter evidence of what other men who had walked abroad this night had already done here. His shoulders sagged, his mattock slipping down along his arm and into the ground at his feet, burying itself lightly into the earth. The old man leaned on it heavily, as though he suddenly could not stand unaided any more.

"They appear to be gone," he whispered brokenly. "But not before they finished their dirty work tonight. Go, you, my boy.

Go, and tell me if what I fear is true. Go, go over there, and tell me what you see."

The boy hesitated, spooked by the way in which his grandfather had apparently aged twenty years or more in the space of a single instant, and then crept forward slowly, his hand tight around his sack.

It was hard to make it all out in the wan moonlight, but he could see enough. The earth looked as if it had been chewed by a hungry dragon, hewed and pitted with small holes, the grass mashed under booted feet and giving off an odor of wounded green, small piles of soil scattered around. Something that looked either makeshift-primitive or broken, obviously an implement used to dig all these holes in the ground, lay discarded a little way off; so did something else, something metallic, something that caught the moonglint and even half hidden by grass and soil gleamed with a pale evil glow. The boy stepped over gingerly to take a better look and saw a folding pocket knife, its blade snapped in half, lying next to something else, something he could not, in the first moment, make out.

And then he did, and frowned.

"They chopped it up," he said, his voice louder than he intended, too loud in the quiet darkness. "They hacked it up— they diced it, and then they seem to have… ground it under their heel…"

The old man lifted his face to the sky, raising one hand, his fingers curled into a savage fist. "Damn you," he said softly. "Damn you all, you bastards, you bandits. You may think you came when nobody was looking but God sees. God knows. Your reward is coming, so help me. It is coming. Are they all gone, boy? All dead? All the bulbs?"

The boy suddenly found that he was crying, without quite knowing why, astonished that he could weep at the death of a few dug-up flower bulbs as though they had been children hewn down by a barbarian invasion. He had not really thought about any of this when his grandfather had hoisted him out of bed that night to come on this expedition. He was of a different generation, all his own experiences being fury and loathing which was more often than not based on the name he bore and not on what or who else he might have been. All he could think of, as he was being shaken awake, was that their bags had been packed for days awaiting their departure, and they were *leaving* this place, leaving behind the fear and hatred that had festered between the two warring peoples who claimed it, one by virtue of history and blood-ties and heartland and the other by right of superior numbers—leaving behind its heavy twin legacies of death and of triumph, finally leaving, finally free—but that was not why his Grandfather had woken him. They were not leaving yet. This place was not done with him yet, and the memories came flooding back.

He remembered his grandmother, gone these many years, with scarlet flowers in her hand. He remembered the way she held them, gently, worshipfully, as though they were precious. He remembered his grandfather coming in out of the summer sunshine and seeing the woman and the flowers and making a sign of blessing upon both. The flowers that grew on this field, and no other. The flowers dyed scarlet by the blood of warriors six hundred years dead. Somehow, he remembered that too— the fierce sounds and stomach-turning stench of ancient battle where blood flowed under swords and horses screamed as they died, and vows were being kept or broken, and a nation hurled itself on the point of history and... what... even six centuries later it was still hard to tell whether they had perished utterly or won themselves a place in the eternal memory of the world. Such is the thin line between heroism and lunacy, between legacy of pride and legacy of hubris. The boy was part of his past, as all men are.

And now, finally, standing here over the shattered bulbs, he suddenly realized what they were and why his grandfather had come here this night.

Standing here, in the open field in the dark hours before his last dawn on the ancestral land for which his forebears had fought and bled and died... he remembered it all, somehow. Remembered the sight and the smell and the bright colour of the blood of a battle that had shaped a nation, blood which had seeped into the ground here and, legend had it, dyed the flower called the *bozur*, which his grandmother had worshipped, to the blood-red which they were to this day.

"All of them?" his grandfather said again. "Is there not one…?"

The boy bent down to bring his eyes closer to the ground, peered at the dug-up earth at his feet. What he could see of the destroyed bulbs made him feel oddly queasy; they looked… wounded, like a human being would have looked wounded. Like a child would have. As though limbs and bones had been hacked apart, as though eyes had been gouged out. Worse—as though these were just potential limbs and bones and eyes. As if he was watching the murder of something yet unborn.

"Would they grow from just a piece of it, grandfather?"

"They may, if it was big enough and not too badly damaged," the old man said. "I don't know. I don't know. Oh, cursed… cursed is the land whose very flowers are damned for existing…"

You should know. This is your blood, your heritage. You should be able to walk on this field and find them without pause, without thinking—this is your heritage, boy.

These were words his grandfather had not uttered out loud to him—not here, not on this field, not this night. But somehow he heard them, clear and carrying like the pealing of the bells in the tower of the orthodox cathedral—another thing they would be leaving when the day broke, a thing that the boy had never even thought about before, not consciously, but which he now missed with a fierceness he had not believed possible—and he had not even left it yet. But the words echoed within him, inside a great empty hollow space. They would be leaving so much that day—that very morning, in fact, and it would be a race for the boy and his grandfather to be back in their home before it was time to leave it forever. They would be leaving… everything behind. Their home. Whatever they could not carry from that home with them in their luggage, in their hands. The bells ringing out from the domed orthodox monasteries and churches built according to plans brought all the way from Byzantium, with now fading frescoes of ancient saints painted nearly a thousand years before. The bones of his grandmother and his father, in their tombs in the church yard. The dog which had grown up with the boy, and which was already handed over to someone else to take care of, a new home, a new home apart.

Their home. Their dead. Their past.

But not all. Dear God, not all. There had to be one left whole. *One*. His grandfather had said that he should be able to tell…

Blindly, with nothing but instinct and memory and pain, the boy fell onto the violated ground and crawled forward on his hands and knees, heedless of the mess the raw earth was making of his clothes, his fingernails crusted with dirt—feeling, questing, reaching out for that part of himself that was buried in this hallowed ground. One. *One*. One had to have survived this senseless destruction—flower bulbs, hacked and destroyed because they were perceived as having a nationality, a bloodline, a legendary provenance which could not be allowed to exist in the new world of the morning—because the new masters of this place could not allow them to exist. Could not allow it because every scarlet bloom that raised its heavy head denied their own right to this place—because they had no connection with a flower that grew only here, and another people did, the people from whom the land had been taken and stolen and wrested and torn, the people whose blood had continued to feed the red flowers for many years while they were systematically hounded and bullied and murdered off their land.

One. *One*. His grandmother's hands had flowed with them once. One had to remain.

He stumbled over a mound of dirt, and his wrist folded, pitching him forward into as yet untrampled grass. He lay there as though dead for a moment, his fingers twisting painfully around two handfuls of grass, his face on the ground, his mouth open and his lips touching the soil as though he was kissing it. And then a strange feeling coursed through him, as though something electric had reached out and burned him. He pushed himself off the ground with one hand, allowing the other to uncurl, to lie flat beside the clump of grass which it had grasped so violently a moment ago. For a moment he sat there, quite still, and then he began to burrow into the soil carefully, using only his hands. He pushed it aside, right and left, gently, his touch as light as if he was caressing his mother's hand.

And then held his breath as something began to emerge from the dirt. An irregular bulb. Unharmed. Whole.

Holy.

He dug around some more, carefully, freeing it from the hold of the earth, and then he stumbled to his feet, his hands dark with dirt, smears of it on his cheek and the corner of his mouth and clinging to his hair, holding something between his palms as a man might hold water in the desert.

"I found one," he whispered. His voice was very soft, almost no more than a breath, but his grandfather's head turned in his direction. The old man said nothing, but his shoulders tensed, and he straightened up, resting only one hand lightly on the mattock.

"I found one," the boy repeated, holding out the bulb.

"Then it is blessing enough," the old man finally said, as though the words were wrung from him. "Bring it. We will make sure the memory lives on."

It was still full night, but away to the east there was the barest hint of a lightening in the sky, the promise of the morning to come. The old man turned to the east and lifted his fist again, a gesture more of a curse than of lamentation now.

"Damn you," he said softly, speaking to the glow in the sky. "Damn all of you who think that killing a flower will kill the memories of a nation. We will survive. We will endure. We leave our bones and our graveyards and our dead behind us, because we must. But we carry the memories within us." He glanced back to where the boy was making his way back with his prize still cradled between his hands like the most precious of jewels. "We will remember," the old man said. "We will remember. As long as that flower blooms. And there will always be one. There will *always* be one."

He allowed his arm to slip briefly around the boy's shoulders as he came near enough, and let his hand convey his pride and his approval, tightening momentarily and then letting go.

"Come," he said. "They will be abroad tonight. And tomorrow, we go. Tomorrow… we go." He swallowed, looking around him at the empty field in the moonlight and shadow, and the boy could see that for the old man it was not empty at all, it was filled with ghosts, with memories, with a long and bitter past. "The best of it... we will take with us," he said softly. "One of them lives."

"I will protect it, grandfather," the boy said, and knew he meant far more than mere words conveyed.

His grandfather understood it, too. Their eyes met, briefly, and then slid apart again.

"Come," the grandfather said, hoisting his mattock back on his shoulder, and deliberately turning back on the violated ground in the field. "Home. Be quiet. Be wary."

They slipped back into the shadows of the trees, and vanished into them.

The breeze stirred the grasses in the Field of Blackbirds, raising a susurrus, a whisper of vanished voices. Ghosts of slain humans and scythed flowers met and mingled in the empty air.

THE WORD BEHIND THE STORY

Saudade (Portuguese): One of the most beautiful of all words, translatable or not, this word refers to the feeling of longing for something or someone that you love and which is lost.

THE STORY BEHIND THE WORD

This story was actually nominated for a Pushcart Prize in the year of its first publication, and the editor who bought it said of it that she could see that it was a story "about something deeply important". It is. There is a flower of the sort described in this tale, and it means exactly this to me, personally—an image, an icon, a living reminder and memory of a lost and precious thing. The very definition of the first step on the road to Saudade.

ABOUT THE AUTHOR

Alma Alexander's life so far has prepared her very well for her chosen career. She was born in a country which no longer exists on the maps, has lived and worked in seven countries on four continents (and in cyberspace!), has climbed mountains, dived in coral reefs, flown small planes, swum with dolphins, touched two-thousand-year-old tiles in a gate out of Babylon. She is a novelist, anthologist and short story writer who currently shares her life between the Pacific Northwest of the USA (where she lives with her husband and two cats) and the wonderful fantasy worlds of her own imagination. You can find out more about Alma on her website (www.AlmaAlexander.org), her Facebook page (https://www.facebook.com/AuthorAlmaAlexander/) or on Twitter (https://twitter.com/AlmaAlexander). You can also support her on Patreon (https://www.patreon.com/AlmaAlexander)

Curious about other Crossroad Press books?
Stop by our site:
http://store.crossroadpress.com
We offer quality writing
in digital, audio, and print formats.

Enter the code FIRSTBOOK
to get 20% off your first order from our store!
Stop by today!

www.ingramcontent.com/pod-product-compliance
Lightning Source LLC
Chambersburg PA
CBHW071133200626
46817CB00018B/2937